"I Want You," [...] With Me To Th[...] House."

Fiona was a little afraid. She'd had no idea he'd come right out and say it. She'd thought he might coax and tease, but he'd said it so deliberately. What did women say now? Probably with him, they'd all said yes. Had any of them said no to him? Could she? At last she shook her head. "I do not dare. I do not trust myself."

"You do not trust *me*." His voice was anguished.

"You must leave me alone," Fiona told him. "I cannot endure this temptation."

"Do you realize what you are doing to me?"

"And what about me?" Fiona said. "Do you think I am enjoying this torment?"

Very softly, his voice deep, he asked, "Is it torment for you?"

"I am not ice," she said.

When Dominic spoke again, his voice was unsteady. "Then let me know your fire."

Dear Reader:

What makes a Silhouette Desire hero? This is a question I often ask myself—it's part of my job to think about these things!—and I *know* it's something you all think about, too. I like my heroes rugged, sexy and sometimes a little infuriating. I love the way our heroes are sometimes just a little bit in the dark about love... *and* about what makes the heroine "tick." It's all part of their irresistible charm.

This March, I want you all to take a good look at our heroes and—if you want—let me know what you think about them!

Naturally, we have a *Man of the Month* who just can't be beat—Dane Lassiter in Diana Palmer's *The Case of the Mesmerizing Boss*. This story is doubly good because not only is it a *Man of the Month* title, it's also the first book in Diana Palmer's new *series,* called MOST WANTED. As for Lassiter, he's a hero you're not likely to ever forget.

Do you think playboys can be tamed? I certainly do! And you can watch one really get his comeuppance in Linda Turner's delightful *Philly and the Playboy*. Barbara McCauley creates a sexy, mountain man (is there any other kind?) in *Man From Cougar Pass,* and Carole Buck brings us a hero who's a bit more citified—but no less intriguing—in *Knight and Day*. And if a seafaring fellow is the type for you, don't miss Donna Carlisle's *Cast Adrift*.

Some heroes—like some real-life men—are less than perfect, and I have to admit I had a few doubts about Lass Small's *Dominic*. But so many of you wrote in asking for his story that I began to wonder if Dominic shouldn't have equal time to state his case. (You'll remember he gave Tate Lambert such a hard time in *Goldilocks and the Behr*.) Is Dominic a hero? I think he very well might be, but I'm interested in hearing what you all thought about this newly tamed man.

So, I've said all I have to say *except* that I do wish you best wishes for happy reading. Now I'm waiting to hear from you.

Until next month,

Lucia Macro
Senior Editor

LASS
SMALL
DOMINIC

SILHOUETTE *Desire*®

Published by Silhouette Books New York

America's Publisher of Contemporary Romance

SILHOUETTE BOOKS
300 East 42nd St., New York, N.Y. 10017

DOMINIC

Copyright © 1992 by Lass Small

All rights reserved. Except for use in any review,
the reproduction or utilization of this work in
whole or in part in any form by any electronic,
mechanical or other means, now known or
hereafter invented, including xerography,
photocopying and recording, or in any information
storage or retrieval system, is forbidden without
the permission of the publisher, Silhouette Books,
300 E. 42nd St., New York, N.Y. 10017

ISBN: 0-373-05697-4

First Silhouette Books printing March 1992

Printed in the U.S.A.

Books by Lass Small

Silhouette Desire

Tangled Web #241
To Meet Again #322
Stolen Day #341
Possibles #356
Intrusive Man #373
To Love Again #397
Blindman's Bluff #413
Goldilocks and the Behr #437
Hide and Seek #453
Red Rover #491
Odd Man Out #505
Tagged #534
Contact #548
Wrong Address, Right Place #569
Not Easy #573
The Loner #594
Four Dollars and Fifty-One Cents #613
No Trespassing Allowed #638
The Molly Q #655
'Twas the Night #684
Dominic #697

*Lambert Series

Silhouette Romance

An Irritating Man #444
Snow Bird #521

Silhouette Books

Silhouette Christmas Stories 1989
"Voice of the Turtles"

LASS SMALL

finds living on this planet at this time a fascinating experience. People are amazing. She thinks that to be a teller of tales of people, places and things is absolutely marvelous.

This book is dedicated to those who search.
My gratitude to Maria Ferrer and to all the people
who wrote to Silhouette asking that Dominic's book
be published.
Thank you.

One

Even before the current ethnic splintering in the United States, the household of Dominic Lorenzo was made up of Italians. Originally, the families had come from around the place of Dominic's own family origin, near the sea, south and west of Rome. So it was not that Dominic was prejudiced, it was just that he preferred his own kind. His people called him Lorenzo.

Hearing his accent, men who Dominic met in business would ask, "Did you immigrate? When did you come to this country?"

"Some time ago," Dominic would reply. No one needed to know the details of his life.

"I'd bet you found school tough, not knowing the language."

He would shrug in a nothing reply.

No one ever mentioned that Dominic Lorenzo hadn't been born in Italy, nor had his parents come from there. They were all actually Chicagoans, but that was a minor detail. For all intent and purpose, the people around Dominic were Italian. They spoke the language in their homes and their social contacts were with their own kind, therefore English was a second language and Dominic's scarce use of it betrayed an accent,

"Are you an equal-opportunity employer?" a woman guest once asked Dominic with some curiosity. He looked like a male chauvinist, the kind a woman wanted for a lover but not at any other time. Male chauvinists were generally sensual and saw to it that a love partner was aroused and eager for his pleasure. The woman thought Dominic Lorenzo looked like that sort of man.

He had looked down her nice body from the shadow of eyelashes that were wicked on such a man. "We have some women in our firm."

A tactful response. Not only did he avoid mentioning that he hired only women who were Italian, but he had said "our" firm. Of course, it was his. He ran it. The decisions were his.

He was a striking example of what can occur in any race. He was exceptionally pleasing to the eye. Michelangelo could have used Dominic's body for the statue of David. A bit taller than average, Dominic had the dark, smoldering good looks of one of the old gods of legend. Noting that with slow, relishing eyes, the family women whispered together and speculated on the Lorenzo woman who had lured one of the legendary myths to seduce her.

Dominic's parents were long dead. He had no siblings. He had been raised in a series of big, noisy Italian families, but he had never felt that he belonged to any of them.

He was a simple man in his habits. He wanted peace, good food, a reasonably tidy house and people to care about. He was also a brilliant businessman, and the strings of power he held in his hand reached far. He was a man of power.

He'd built his own agri-business, which dealt in grains and those derived products. He'd been aggressive in a fortuitous time of flux development and had solidified his contacts.

His wealth was sobering. Monied peoples attract scavengers who will use any means to rip away shares of that wealth. Like others who have that burden, Dominic became a recluse to protect himself and those he loved. Above all, family was sacred.

Oddly enough, Dominic was twice-divorced, but worse, his wives had not been Italian. It was a puzzle for such a man to commit to something as serious as marriage with two women who were not of his kind. And for such a virile man he had fathered but one child, a son whose name was Benjamin.

Every Italian knows his sons must be raised in the family, to know of their responsibilities, their connections and the way of their lives. It was a fact. And Dominic had his son.

The woman who cared for Benjamin was Maria Evans. Dominic could bend. He trusted Maria Garibaldi, even if her last name was Evans. She, too, had married outside their kind. However, her Italian speech was perfect and her English equally skilled, but her marriage hadn't flawed her—she thought as an Italian would. And she loved Benjamin.

Maria played with Benjamin as if he was her own child. At almost fifty, she was supple and filled with laughter. But on that late summer's day, she was watching the child instead of the grade of the land. She tripped, lost her footing and fell heavily.

Benjamin ran to her, and the three-year-old was smart enough to know that Maria wasn't teasing. "You are hurt!"

"Yes-s-s," Maria hissed through pain-clenched teeth in the prerequisite Italian. "Call Tomas. Go fetch Romano. Go carefully."

But Benjamin ran all the way.

For Romano to see Dominic's son come running, unattended, was to strike terror into his loyal heart. He snatched the boy up to his wide chest for protection and turned his shielding back to any pursuers as he took giant steps to the safety of the house. Romano *knew* Maria had thrown herself into the breach and prevented Benjamin's kidnapping. Where was their guard Tomas?

"Maria." Benjamin pointed back, over Romano's shoulder.

But Romano was shouting and didn't hear.

"Maria." Benjamin insisted. "Hurt."

"Yes," Romano soothed distractedly. Even shouting for reserves of housemen and yardmen, Romano knew that if anything had happened to Maria, Ned Evans would not only have Tomas's still-beating heart clenched in his hand, but all of their gullets as well, torn raw from their throats. Romano had always thought that Ned Evans would have made a fine Italian.

So it was a while before Benjamin got their attention enough so that they knew Maria had fallen and was hurt. With a command that would have made his father blink with envy, Benjamin had insisted the men take him back to Maria, but they would not. He was sent with the cook to the upper floor while most of the men stayed below. Then Romano and two others cautiously went in search of whatever had happened. They knew they went to find Maria's body.

She was not only alive, she was being firm with Tomas that he was not to move her until someone came who knew what he was doing. So they all argued and shouted, but finally Romano called the EMS on his cordless phone.

The emergency crew was patient with the shakedown Romano put them through when they arrived at the gate, and they were finally admitted onto the Lorenzo grounds.

There, the medical crew mentioned in English, and in a really very snide way, that they were lucky the patient hadn't bled to death while she had to wait for care. They agreed with her the problem was her hip and that it was probably broken. Why had she jumped from that ledge? Finally Maria was carefully taken to the hospital. Her hip was broken.

Before Maria was given the initial sedative, and Tomas was still with her, she told him firmly in Italian, "Call Fiona. She is to go to Benjamin. I say so."

So the call came to Fiona at an office in downtown Chicago near the river. In early times, the city fathers had made the river flow backward so that the dumped sewage would be sent away from Lake Michigan. The cleaner river was now lined with office buildings, and the building in which Fiona worked was one.

The business was a service operation. Whatever needed doing by anyone in a vacation house, or an office, or with a visiting personage who needed anything—that was moral and legal—the office would provide it. Care and supply led to some interesting scrambles.

Being one of the few actual natives of Chicago, Fiona was extremely good at locating odd items that were suddenly vital to someone's health or welfare. And she didn't get frazzled.

She was twenty-six, tall, Italian-dark with blue-green eyes. She was stunning. Men's stares were drawn to her, but she wasn't interested. She was probably more Evans than Garibaldi, but she did rally to the flag in any emergency.

When Romano called, Fiona replied in Italian, "I'll go now." Then in English, she told her boss. "It's an emergency. My mother is hurt."

Kevin McBride frowned at Fiona and asked, "Car wreck?"

"A fall. Her hip is broken."

"Sorry. How can I help?" Kevin was thinking that this might give him a toehold with the luscious bit of elusive Italian confection who made his mouth water just to look at her.

Fiona wrote hurriedly on a piece of paper as she said, "There's nothing that can be done. Thanks. I'll be in touch."

"Are you going to the hospital? I could take you." Kevin stood up.

"No." She handed him the slip of paper. "Here is the number of my cousin, Angelina. She knows where everything is, in Chicago. We have used her before.

She can fill in for me until I get back. I must go to
Benjamin."

"I thought your father's name was Ned."

"It is." Fiona was distracted. "I must go."

And Fiona left. Just like that. She vanished. Kevin
frowned. Who was Benjamin?

At Dominic Lorenzo's compound Fiona knew to
stop her car, because she had substituted for her
mother before in caring for Benjamin. Fiona was
greeted with the usual male interest, but added to that
was compassion for her mother's injury. However,
even knowing Fiona and even being her mother's
daughter, Fiona had to be checked out thoroughly, but
with respect.

Fiona understood all that. In Italian, she asked,
"Where is Romano?"

"At the house, like a mother hen. He is baby-sitting
Benjamin. He will not let the boy out of the house."

"A man of dedication." She agreed. She then
frowned because the gate watcher laughed.

As Fiona drove up the lane, she remembered that
Romano was a truly dedicated man. He had eleven
children. Last count. An emancipated woman, Fiona
shook her head in disapproval. Eleven children were
a kick in the teeth to this overpopulated world.

In the compound, the Lorenzo house was not os-
tentatious. It was discreetly set along the western
shoreline of Lake Michigan in the northern part of
Chicago.

The main residence had once been a summer home.
The other houses in that segment had been bought at
the same time and most had been demolished. Those

left were the homes of the Lorenzo staff. Dominic Lorenzo could afford to do something like that.

But it was perfect. The surrounding iron fence was so artfully contrived that the unlikelihood of scaling it was concealed. On the enclosed grounds, all the asphalt and empty cement basements had been dug out, removed and filled with earth. The extra trees had then been planted in the natural, rather haphazard way.

The lane to the house was a country lane, the waters of the lake could be seen between the tree trunks, and the summer's foliage was thick and healthy. Only the muted sounds of traffic gave any clue that the place was a part of a very large city.

The sprawling house was frame, comfortable, with large windows cunningly covered with delicate grillwork to disguise the fact that the place was a fortress. The porches were large and easy. There were porch swings and fan-backed chairs that looked very homey. But it all camouflaged the shadow men who watched as they lounged or walked among the clutter of hanging ferns and large potted plants.

Fiona pulled her car into the visitors space and walked back to the porch.

"So." Speaking in the Italian used on the compound, she addressed the guard whose name was Nick. "You are still running loose and free? Or has that little blonde, Anita, tied you in knots?"

"She is working on it." His manner was smug, but his sharp gaze covered the area beyond the porch.

"Does she know what she is doing? You would keep her barefoot and pregnant."

"Just so." And Nick grinned, his eyes twinkled, wickedly humorous.

"I need to speak with her." Fiona sighed and shook her head.

"She listens only to me."

"It is biology. It is not true love," Fiona warned. "What do you two talk about?"

"Who talks?" He shrugged, but he was looking beyond her, his eyes moving as he watched.

Again Fiona vowed, "I need to speak with her."

"An old maid like you? What can you tell her?" Nick raised his eyebrows and waited, his alert awareness of the area never wavering.

Fiona flung out an arm toward the trees. "About the whole world that lies beyond the kitchen and bedroom."

He laughed. "You need a man."

"I have not seen one who would be worth the time."

"You will." He moved to see along another angle.

"How certain you are." Fiona sighed with impatience. "How narrow-visioned. I shall speak to Anita."

"Go ahead. She will laugh." Then his glance came back to Fiona briefly before he told her, "Benjamin came alone to the house to get help for your mother."

"Ahh." Her heart was touched. Fiona went into the silent house. "Benjamin?" she called.

Upstairs, there was the sound of a child's running feet and Benjamin yelled in his father's language, "Fiona! Fiona? Are you here?"

She laughed and called, "Yes."

The cherub stood, then, at the top of the stairs. A three-year-old Pluto, a dark angel smiling down on Fiona in a blessing. "You are here." He said that in great satisfaction. Then he sobered. "Maria?"

"She is at the hospital." Fiona's Italian words were to reassure. "They are giving care to her."

His face sad, Benjamin said, "She was hurt." His words were thought out and said individually as he chose them.

"She will be all right." Fiona was positive. "She sent me to be with you."

He smiled again. "I am glad."

"Come down."

Benjamin told her, "Romano says to stay here."

"Romano?" Fiona called.

Footsteps came along the upper hall. He greeted Fiona with the fact, "You are here."

"As you see. May Benjamin come down the stairs? All is clear." Fiona took a deep, appreciating breath. "And I can smell that lunch is almost ready."

"Yes?" Benjamin looked up at the big man.

It was obvious the man took his work very seriously. He nodded once. "He may."

Benjamin came down the steps one at a time, sliding a holding hand along the railing. "You are here!" he said again to Fiona. "We will sing and laugh."

"Yes." Fiona watched him. "You do very well on the stairs."

Benjamin chose his words carefully. "My legs are still too short."

Fiona was tender with the impatient little boy. "The time will come when your legs are as long as Romano's."

That man quietly went on by them now that Benjamin was almost down the stairs. Romano had tactfully kept his descent equal to the child's.

"No." Benjamin corrected her. "Long, like Papa's."

Fiona had never met Dominic. There were no pictures of him in the house. He was a mysterious man who avoided publicity or interviews. For all the world knew of him, he could be a mirage. A conglomerate? Fiona smiled at the idea. That would be a clever ruse: a committee that was called Dominic Lorenzo.

Like any male who is conscious of his place in the world, Benjamin stopped on the steps while his face was still level with Fiona's. From that equal height, he smiled at her and said, "I am glad to see you."

"Thank you. And thank you for taking care of my mother."

"You are welcome," he replied solemnly. Then he came down the stairs and took her hand. "Would you take lunch with me?"

Rather pensively, Fiona told him, "When you are sixteen, you will be the terror of all mothers who have beautiful daughters."

Since adults tend to say unfathomable things to children, Benjamin accepted that as another such comment. If what Fiona said was important, she would simplify it for him in order for him to understand. Fiona was good at explaining. She was nice to him. He liked her.

They went down the center hall at Benjamin's pace and turned the corridor to the kitchen wing of the house. There ruled a stoutly comfortable woman of mature years. She could be any age either side of fifty. She was a superb cook who served attractive meals, taking the time to make the table pleasing. Everyone called this childless woman "Momma." She accepted that.

She was serene and ever busy. She customarily wore a gray dress and a white bib apron. She had drop gold earrings in her ears that waggled and wiggled with her movements. She wore no makeup, and her black, black hair was drawn tightly back into a small bun.

Momma had two younger women to assist her with the lesser meals. More aides would be used for dinner and for holiday meals. The two helpers were silent, quick and obedient. They did not miss a thing.

"So, Momma." Fiona greeted the lady. And she smiled to acknowledge the silent head nods of the welcoming assistants.

"Fiona." Momma greeted the guest. "Tomas called. Your mother is still being fixed. They are doing it carefully. Your father is there and he is fine. No need for you to go to him. 'Stay with Benjamin,' he tells you. And he said you are to know that Tomas will be with him. Are you in distress?"

"A little. It is better that I am here. Papa will be surrounded by family, Garibaldis and Evanses. It is kind of Tomas to stay there, but there is no need."

"Lorenzo said to do it in that way."

"I am here because my mother told me to come to Benjamin," Fiona reminded Momma. "I am here for just today."

Momma turned and looked at Fiona rather belligerently, then she said, "Tomas will be with your father in your place. Tomas will take that very seriously. He is a good man."

"I shall tell him that you say so."

At the stove, Momma hesitated in filling a bowl as she considered Fiona's words. Then Momma nodded once and agreed, "You may tell him, this one time."

Fiona laughed softly, and Momma raised inquiring eyebrows at Fiona as if she were not aware why Fiona should laugh.

Fiona said, "Someone must come to be with Benjamin. I have work. I cannot be away from it for too long."

Momma frowned and said, "Sit, sit. Benjamin, have you washed your hands?"

"Yes, ma'am." He gave her his cherub look.

Momma eyed him severely. "You have not. Go and do it." Then she shot Fiona a stare and added, "You, also."

Fiona looked down at Benjamin, who was grinning, and she whispered in English, "How'd she know?"

Benjamin chortled.

They went into the bath off the library, where there was a step stool by the lavatory so that Benjamin could wash his own hands. Fiona shared the soap and complimented him on what a good job he had done. He gave her a quick, sharing look of humor.

Fiona sighed as, in Italian, she added to her previous observations, "Probably two or even three *generations* of daughters who will all have prematurely gray-haired mothers."

Another of the senseless statements of the adults.

It was very difficult to eat just a moderate amount. The men ate with such gusto, such smackings and murmurings of pleasure, that the competitive streak in Fiona did surface, but she was of staunch character. Full, but not quite to gluttony, she and Benjamin finally left the table and went out onto the back porch. There they sat in the rockers reserved for the kitchen people. The staff was busy and the rockers needed to be reminded how to rock, Fiona told Benjamin.

He could understand that.

He rocked himself to sleep.

Romano came outside onto the porch to check on them and smiled down on the sleeping boy, nodding in satisfaction. "I take him up."

"Mother says he is not sleeping at night. She has been trying to keep him awake during the day, with only a little nap, so that he will sleep at night."

"Where do you want him?"

"In the library for a little while? On the sofa there? We shall let him sleep about forty-five minutes. Then I will waken him for a walk?"

"Why do you not call the hospital and speak with your papa?"

"Thank you. I shall do so." She stood up.

Romano gently scooped the child up from the chair and carried his small burden through the door Fiona held open for him.

She went ahead and spread an afghan on the sofa. Romano laid the boy down. Benjamin was sleeping so soundly that he didn't even move.

Fiona adjusted him so that he was comfortable. Then she put a light summer wool throw over him. The breeze from the lake was fresh.

She called the hospital and talked to her dad in English, of course. He only knew love words and swear words in Italian. She asked him, "How are you? Are you all right?"

He groused. "Tomas plays a mean game of gin."

"What about Mother?"

Her dad sighed. "They've still got her in there. Somebody comes out now and then tells me everything is all right. I hate this."

"Do you want me there?" Her voice had gone up several notches.

"Naw," he reassured her. "You play a rotten no-challenge game of gin."

"You know what I mean," Fiona said urgently. "Should I come down there?"

"No, honey, don't pay any attention to me. I don't sit still very well. There's a flock of relatives around, and Tomas treats me like I'm something he's responsible for. He's a nice kid. We're doing okay. You stay with Benjamin. I'll see you tonight. Oh, I forgot, you're staying there tonight."

"No." Fiona frowned at the wall. "I'll come by the hospital on my way home."

They finished the inane conversation that was only to reassure each other, and finally they said goodbye and hung up. Fiona sat with her hand on the phone. Why would her father say she was staying at the compound? At lunch, Momma had said something like that, too. Why would they assume that she was spending the night?

Her mother was hired to be there only during the day, and she really liked Benjamin. She read to him and instructed him in speaking English and Italian. And she played with him. But she did not stay at the compound at night.

Fiona got up and went back to the library. She looked down at Benjamin sleeping so hard. Fiona liked him, too. She smiled down at the little boy. He had another twenty-five minutes to sleep before she wakened him and took him outside so that he could get tired enough to sleep all night long. Three-year-olds were notorious for prowling during the night and dropping off into naps here and there during the day. It was another way kids had of driving parents to exhaustion.

Fiona sat down in a very comfortable chair to rest for that twenty minutes. The house was silent. There were only the distant, soothing sounds of muted traffic, of the waves along the shore and of the breeze stirring in the leaves. It was very peaceful and she went sound asleep.

So it was that Dominic Lorenzo found them. He stood and looked at his son, then he glanced over at the woman... the girl. So this was Maria's daughter.

He went over and stood in front of her, and since she was sound asleep he was free to really look at her without her knowing. She was very, very lovely. Her dark hair was just a bit untidy. Small strands were loosened from the knot at the back of her neck and they curled by her ears and along her temples.

Her skin was pale. Her eyelashes were long and thick and lay fanned on her cheeks concealing her eyes. What color were they?

He looked down at her. Her hands were lax on her lap. Beautiful, graceful—ringless—hands. And her breasts were soft pillows. Her feet were placed so that her knees were together; her ankles were fragile.

And he felt the stir of desire.

For this child? No. She was not a child, she was a woman. This was Fiona Evans, Maria's daughter. She was twenty-six and had a master's degree in marketing. She might look like an untried child, but she was old enough to have lost that innocent look. And he wondered how many lovers she had had.

The thought of some man putting his hands on that lax body was disturbing to Dominic. His gaze went over her sleeping form, and his hands curled.

He looked away from her, out of the window. That was no help. His body was aware she lay back, relaxed in his chair, right there before him.

Dominic found he wanted to kneel down, take her in his arms and press his face into the soft mounds of her breasts. He wanted to begin by kissing her.

He could not justify an affair with Maria's daughter. He would avoid her. That was what he would do. He would not see her and their paths would not cross. That would be easy.

But his feet did not move. He stood there by her sleeping form, watching her, and he was disturbed by the wanting of her.

Two

Fiona dreamed. She dreamed she was a mermaid lying indolent in a warm sea, and the waves that lapped at her were sensual ones, disturbing her in secret places. Then she became aware that a great seal man was lying on a rock, watching her. There could be no mating between a mermaid and a seal man. Wasn't that so? Then why did she yearn? With her eyes closed and lying immobile in the somnolent waves, why did she feel his gaze was on her in lust?

She frowned just a little and twitched to swim away, but she was oddly caught in a . . . net? She gasped in alarm, and the seal man slid into the water with little swishing sounds as he disappeared, and she was again very alone in the empty seas as she had been for eons.

She wakened sadly, in a strange grief for losing—

Fiona saw that she was in the Lorenzo home, in the library, in a chair. She had been asleep. Her mind clawed to regather the dream which faded in wisps that were lost. So she was left with a vague melancholy she didn't understand at all. She frowned at the pain of losing . . . a dream. It was only a dream. How silly.

She sat silently, dismissing the nonsense of a seal man. A seal man! Ridiculous.

She looked over at the sleeping Benjamin. Then she glanced at her watch. Good grief! She had slept an hour. Benjamin would never sleep the night through now. Poor night sitter.

Going over to the boy, she said in English, "Hey, lazybones, what are you doing still asleep?"

He replied also in English, "I woke up once, but you were asleep." He smiled wickedly. "I didn't want to wake you up. So I was quiet."

She laughed out loud.

"I need a cookie."

"We'll ask Momma." Fiona took him into the bathroom first.

In the kitchen, Momma said in Italian, "You will spend the night. Lorenzo says the boy needs security. He said this. He has spoken with your father, who agreed."

Fiona couldn't believe it. In English, she protested, "I didn't agree. I have a job. I need to go home. I need clothes for tomorrow. I need to see my mother." What business did her father have, committing her to doing anything? Her temper sparked.

In Italian, Momma responded. "Nick went to your house and brought back some of your clothes."

In a mild explosion, Fiona's one word burst. "What?"

Momma eyed Fiona as if she were not too bright. "Your clothes are in the room next to Benjamin's."

In English, Fiona enunciated the words. "I didn't give permission to anyone to move my things around, and I didn't agree to stay anywhere. I am an adult. I have a job. I need to go to work."

In her own language, Momma retorted, "Your boss, who is Kevin McBride—what a strange name—he has been informed."

"By whom?" Fiona was direly serious in Italian.

"By your father. I told you that Lorenzo spoke with your father."

Through her teeth, Fiona informed Momma in English, "My father doesn't tell me what to do."

Lifting her nose, Momma replied in Italian, "He did not. Lorenzo did."

Also in Italian, Fiona said stridently, "I cannot and will not stay tonight. Get someone."

"You are being difficult," Momma informed the malcontent.

"I said it. Do it." Fiona stared Momma down.

And Momma tried to hide a smile.

With their cookies and a bottle of fruit juice to share, the three-year-old and his companion went outside to see if they could counterbalance an extra forty minutes of sleep with good exercise.

They played and ran and laughed. They explored. Benjamin showed Fiona where her mother had fallen that morning. And after that Fiona wasn't so free.

From the woods, Dominic Lorenzo watched the subdued Fiona. He had seen her look back at the drop where her mother had fallen. He returned to the house and called to Nick. Dominic said to Nick, "Ready the small car. Miss Evans will be going to the hospital to see her mother." Then he showered, dressed and left the compound.

When the trampers came back to the house, Fiona found only Romano. In Italian she informed Romano, "I must leave."

"Nick will drive you to the hospital."

"I am going home. I can drive myself." She was firm.

"Your car needed servicing. It has been taken to the garage."

"By whose order?"

He smiled. "Lorenzo's."

"It is my car. I did not give permission for it to be serviced. Return it."

"But—"

"Now." Her voice was very calm.

He grumbled almost silently, "I do not know why women will make such a disturbance—"

"I want my car."

"Peace, peace. I will call." He left and came back in a very short time to say, "They found some bad spots. It had to be gutted and is up on a rack. The mechanics have left. It cannot be repaired until tomorrow." He made a helpless gesture.

"Where is Lorenzo?"

Romano shrugged. "He did not tell us where he was going."

"He is not here?"

"No."

Fiona took a deep and dangerous breath. "You cannot tell me that he does not leave a number where he can be contacted."

Grudgingly Romano said, "Only in an emergency."

"This—" she said emphatically "—this is an emergency."

Romano knew it was time to placate. "I will call." Then he turned back. "Lorenzo will not take kindly to this interruption."

"If he goes to jail on charges of white slavery, his whole life will be interrupted."

"It is not wise to anger Lorenzo," Romano cautioned.

"It is less wise to anger me!"

Did that frighten Romano? No. He muttered to the ceiling, as if asking for patience, then he left the room.

"Has Romano made you...angry?" Benjamin had to search for the word.

Fiona straightened her back to stretch up her neck so that her head turned like a guard mere mouse in Africa. She replied parsimoniously, "Somewhat."

"I see Papa angry." Benjamin considered that fact. "He does it ... well."

"I imagine that is so." She bent her neck to acknowledge that.

"Tomas says Papa ... puffs fire, like a dragon."

Fiona said softly, but in a meticulous manner, "So do I."

Benjamin watched her, waiting, quite curious, not at all alarmed.

A corner of Fiona's mind was intrigued by that. Benjamin had watched Dominic in an angry mood, but he had not frightened the boy. Interesting.

Romano came into the room and went over to pick up a phone to hold it out to Fiona. "He will speak to you."

Fiona noted that Romano's eyes sparkled with indulgent humor. She took the phone and in her most intimidating manner and in English, she said, "I want my car back, now."

"Ah, Miss Evans," he said in Italian. "Romano has prepared the small car to take you to visit your mother, now. Thank you for staying tonight with Benjamin. Let Romano or Momma know if there is anything that you need."

And he hung up.

Fiona gasped, then turned to Romano to shout in Italian, "I want to talk to him! He hung up!"

"He does that."

She snarled, "Call him back! What is the number?"

Very gently Romano explained, "He would not answer. He has solved it to his satisfaction."

Fiona clenched her fists and bit her lower lip. "I am not in his employ. He has stolen my car and—"

Nick came into the room. "The car is ready. Would you like to go now?"

Slowly she turned to Nick. "My car?"

"No." He glanced over at Romano. "It is the small car. I will take you to see your mother."

"As soon as I pack." She whirled to her left and stalked across the room.

Romano's voice was very kind. "You cannot leave Benjamin here alone all night."

"He has a father." She paused at the door and looked back coldly.

Romano opened his hands. "He is not here."

"He is an autocrat."

"I know not that word."

In English she expanded it. "He gets his own way."

Romano nodded slowly, as if he'd known that all along.

Fiona then looked at Benjamin. He was such a little boy. He'd run all the way to the house to get help for her mother that very morning. She said to him, "I am going to see my mother at the hospital. Would you draw a little picture for her?"

"Will you come back and stay with me?"

She gave it up. "Yes."

Benjamin laughed and the two men chuckled.

She gave them all a scathing glance and left the room. She went up the stairs and into the room next to Benjamin's. It wasn't a woman's room. It was Dominic's? She looked into the closet. It was his. She stood and looked around more slowly. It wasn't luxurious. The bed was quite large and long.

She went slowly out of the room, back into the hallway, and went to the room on the other side of Benjamin's. She wondered what Dominic Lorenzo looked like. Yes. A picture she'd once seen. The World War II dictator, Mussolini, with his big chin. That was probably quite accurate.

In the other room, her makeup and brushes were laid out on the dresser, as if she had lived there for a long time. If it had been Nick who had moved her, he had experience. He had remembered exactly where she had placed those things on her dresser at home.

Fiona opened the closet. Her things hung perfectly. There was one of her cases on a luggage stand, and in it were her undergarments. He had not touched them. He had to have touched them to pack them, but he pretended he hadn't by not unpacking them. Interesting.

She showered and put on fresh clothing. It was late summer and oddly cool now and then by the lake. She took up a jacket and went back downstairs.

Benjamin had finished an elaborate drawing. Fiona sat down and said, "Tell me about it."

It was the story of her mother falling and being carried away in a truck. Fiona labeled the places that weren't clear. "It is a good picture," she told the boy.

"Tell her to get well."

"I will."

"And—" he watched Fiona "—come back."

"Yes."

"Momma set out Benjamin's supper," Romano told Fiona. "I will feed him."

"I feed me," Benjamin corrected.

"Like his father." Romano smiled at Fiona.

She looked down her nose at them. "Like all of you." She informed them in English.

The men laughed indulgently.

The "small" car was a ponderous black thing. It wasn't a limo, nothing that obvious or attention-gathering. Disgruntled, Fiona looked at the car. It was probably bullet-proof. Nick opened the door with a flourish. He was so pleased to be the driver that she could not be sour about it. She thanked him and got into the thing.

The taped music was Italian opera. Fiona wondered why Dominic didn't just move to Italy? This was America. He ought to adjust to being assimilated. When in Rome, do as the Romans...uh...well. Living here, Dominic ought to act more like an American.

Look at his compound. The others were all Italian and they all spoke Italian. The food was Italian. The car wasn't, but the music was. Fiona thought Lorenzo carried the Italian part much too far.

The heavy black car drew some attention as they came to the hospital. Nick drove up to the curb in a no-parking zone. Heads turned. It would seem to Fiona that if Lorenzo wanted to be anonymous, he wouldn't drive around in such a car. Or would he?

She waited as Nick jumped out, came around and helped her out. He wasn't deterred by the fact that he was in a no-parking zone. He left the car there. She felt the need to say, in Italian, "I do not need your escort. You must park somewhere else." She pointed. "No parking."

He grinned. "That sign is for peasants."

He took her to the elevators and to the correct floor. There, crowding the waiting area were unmixed Garibaldis and Evanses. They all nodded and smiled, hugged and kissed her. The Garibaldis did that with emotion; the Evanses were more discreet. All were tired. Her father was asleep, sprawled at one end of a couch. Tomas was watching over him. Tomas smiled and said, "Your mother is well. She is in her room. I shall get the nurse. You may see her."

Fiona wondered if the permission was Tomas's or if the hospital agreed. She leaned down and kissed her father's forehead, then followed Tomas several steps to hear Nick tell her, "I will see to your father."

She looked back, surprised. "Thank you."

He bowed his head once, quite formally. Then he straightened and moved about, looking around.

Fiona wondered if the Lorenzo people realized other people just went about their own business? They did not need protection. And her father would be ticked off if he realized they were protecting him. From what? He took care of himself, his wife and his daughters.

Fiona saw that the nurse stole quick glances over Tomas as they walked down the corridor. Tomas did not appear to notice that. He stopped outside the door in the hallway as Fiona followed the nurse into her mother's room. There the nurse told her patient bracingly, "Mrs. Evans, you have company."

Maria opened her eyes lazily. She had tubes running into her, and something on the bottom of her nose to give her oxygen.

It was a jolt to Fiona to see her mother in that situation. Fiona felt her own bravery waver, but she stiffened her spine and gently took her mother's hand. "I love you."

Her mother focused on her and smiled. Then she closed her eyes.

The nurse said, "You can stay five minutes. She really doesn't need company. Seeing her is to reassure you. She's fine. It was a nasty break, but the doctor did brilliantly. The surgical nurses are still talking about it."

It was nice to speak in English. Fiona said, "I'm glad the doctor was available." Then she handed the nurse Benjamin's drawing, as she explained, "This is a picture from Benjamin for my mother. He's three years old. He was with mother—"

"Take care of Benjamin." Her eyes closed, her mother said that softly in English.

Fiona swung her head around and stared at her mother in some indignation, then she looked at the nurse and asked suspiciously, "Was Lorenzo up here?" Why else would her mother make the effort to say that in her condition?

"Lorenzo?" The nurse tried to remember.

Fiona waved a hand to erase her query. "It doesn't matter."

The nurse smiled. "You can come back later, if you like."

"Is my dad all right?"

The nurse nodded. "That man with him is just darling. I wish I had someone like him to look after me."

"Flirt with him."

"I tried," the nurse admitted. "He does see me, but he doesn't speak English. He is devoted to caring for your father. Is he some relation?"

"No."

The nurse considered that. Then she said, "You don't have to wait for visiting hours tomorrow. You may come up in the morning. Your mother will be groggy for a day or so. She's on painkillers now. As she's taken off those, she'll be more alert but less comfortable for a while. It will be nice if you could be around more then."

"I don't like to see her suffer." Fiona frowned.

"Think of it as getting well."

"You're very positive." Fiona considered her.

The nurse explained casually, "I've seen miracles. And the work on your mother's hip was exceptional. They did a remarkable job. She should have a full recovery and go running off that ledge again...knowing it's there and not stumbling."

Fiona smiled. "I'm glad you're with her."

The nurse grinned back. "We all do our best."

Fiona leaned to kiss her mother's forehead, then moved away to go to the door, pausing, looking back at her mother.

The nurse said kindly, "We'll take good care of her."

"I know. She's just never needed any care before this."

"I have a mother like that."

Fiona was positive. "They're supposed to stay that way."

Her father was still sleeping heavily. Fiona could not bring herself to waken him, as much as she needed him to hug her in reassurance. She asked an aunt, "Tell him I was here?"

While the aunt nodded, it was Tomas who replied in Italian, "I will."

She looked at Tomas and smiled just a little, because he had allowed the nurse to believe he didn't understand English. In Italian she replied, "We appreciate you."

"I do this for Maria, but it was Lorenzo who has allowed me to be here."

Him again.

Then, knowing how Dominic bullied his way, Fiona assured Tomas, "You could leave." She gestured at all the relatives there. "They are here."

"I stay."

"There is a nurse who has an appreciation for you." She teased Tomas.

"That one." He motioned with his head. "The one who went into Maria's room with you. I know. She does not speak our language."

"To-mos." Fiona was very patient. "You can speak English perfectly well."

He disparaged that. "Only when I must speak to someone who does not understand our language."

"She cannot."

"I know." Tomas spared Fiona a small glance. "I told her that her... figure was womanly. She did not react, and asked what had I said."

"Shame on you."

He looked at her from under lowered eyelashes and smiled just a little. How male. How like one of Dominic's men.

Nick escorted Fiona back down to that cumbersome car, and a police officer patiently waited beside it. Nick said to Fiona, "Be silent. If you must speak, speak only Italian." He carefully put Fiona into the back seat while the officer waited.

"Good evening, officer. Thank you for guarding the car," Nick said in Italian. He opened the car door to get into the driver's seat.

"Stop." The officer spoke Italian.

Nick laughed. "Ahh, you look German. How do you come to speak the language?"

"My papa. You can read that sign, or you are driving without a license. Either way, you get a ticket. Let me see your license."

Nick shrugged. "Win some, lose some." He said that in English.

But it gave Fiona a feeling of satisfaction that one of those bullheaded male chauvinists had had a setback. If Nick had just found a ticket on his windshield, it would have helped her feeling of frustration. But Nick had tried to sneak by the cop so blandly that to have Nick hauled up short was satisfying. She did not like people who nudged aside the laws to suit themselves.

Nick returned the car to the compound, with Fiona intact. With her mother's admonition to care for Benjamin, Fiona was resigned to staying in Dominic's house.

Dominic did not return to the compound until almost two the next morning. He nodded to the shadows who moved so that he knew the men were alert to him and he was being monitored. He went quietly into the house and turned as he closed the door silently. He heard singing. It was an English nursery song. He followed the sound and stood back from the darkened doorway. It was she.

She sat in his big chair, where she had slept that afternoon. Benjamin lay across her lap, his head on her shoulder. He was holding one of his feet in an idle way, and he was singing along with a word here and there.

In the soft light of the lamp her hair was loose around her shoulders in soft waves, with occasional, unexpected little ducktails at the ends. She wore a long gown and a soft velvet robe of lavender. Her feet were bare. He wanted to take them into his hot hands and warm them.

The thought startled Dominic and he frowned.

He looked at her harder, more critically, and she was exquisite. He was jealous of his son's lax body lying so close to her softness.

Benjamin let go of his foot and it sank down onto her thigh. His hand slid over her arm to hang free as he went to sleep.

Dominic watched as she smiled down at his son. But she did not move. Benjamin was probably too heavy for her to lift and carry up the stairs. Was she waiting for one of the men who came through the house on their rounds?

Dominic didn't want any of the men to see her in that lavender robe with her feet bare that way. He moved so that she looked up, surprised. She had not expected to see anyone. She was not waiting to be seen. He smiled at her and said softly in Italian, "He has been prowling at night, eh?"

She was mesmerized. This was Lorenzo. That dratted old dictator was this magnificent man. Lorenzo. He was not old, he was probably thirty-seven or around there. He was beautifully male, and he was the embodiment of power. He walked that way, as he came toward her. He had spoken. She could not remember what he had said. She needed to reply or seem like a dolt. She said, "Sh-h-h." She had just told Dominic to hush?

He smiled.

Something shivered down under her arms, over her breasts and into her stomach. It was a strange feeling. It was like being deliciously scared.

Her eyes looked enormous. They were blue-green and her lashes were as black as her hair. Her mouth was sweet. Her lips were parted. He knew what she would look like in his bed.

This was Maria's daughter.

"Shall I take him up now?" His words were Italian.

She nodded, looked down at the boy and opened her arms.

A swamping wave of desire went through him, and his lips opened to take in a sharp breath.

Since Dominic had not leaned down yet, Fiona looked up and their gazes locked. It was very strange. Then she looked down at the boy again. Still rocked by the feelings that shot frizzles through her, she managed to whisper, "Be careful. He's just asleep. Don't jostle him, or we'll be up another hour."

"That nap this afternoon?" He smiled as he shared the knowledge, and that he had caught her sleeping, too.

Her startled gaze came up to his and she thought . . .
the seal man! And she remembered the dream man
disappearing in little swishes . . . Dominic's footsteps
on the carpet! He had seen her. And then she remembered the longing of the mermaid who had been herself.

Dominic bent over and carefully slid the back of his
hand just under her breasts as he carefully scooped
Benjamin from her body. His other hand moved along
her hip and over her stomach. She was tautly soft, and
he was completely unaware of his son as he concentrated on the feeling of his forearm touching, pushing
up her breasts in slow motion as he lifted the small
boy.

With his touchings, she was stunned by the sensations that now rioted inside her body and along her
skin's surface. It was weird. It was thrilling. It was
astounding. She was panting and a little disoriented.

He had lifted the boy and was holding him across
his arms. Dominic was breathing rather harshly, as if
he labored with that small task. He had turned away
and looked back over his shoulder at her, still sitting
there, but curled forward and seeming a bit disorganized. He said, "I shall come back for you. This has
been a bad day for you. You must be very tired."

The idea of Dominic actually carrying her up to her
bed almost made her swoon. She put a hand to her
forehead to see if her head was still on straight, got
control and stood up.

He felt a strong disappointment. Slowly he moved
toward the door, but waited until she opened it wider.
He could have done that with his shoulder, but he
wanted her—attending him. He smiled at her.

Tying her robe firmly, she went ahead of him, up the stairs to ready Benjamin's bed.

Dominic thought if Benjamin wakened again, it would be easy for him stay up with the boy and watch Fiona. That was her name, Fiona. Fiona, who was Maria's daughter.

He walked into Benjamin's room and laid him very carefully onto his bed. He looked around the room, then he looked at Fiona.

If life went as it was supposed to go, she would now say, Make love to me.

She said, "Good night." Then she walked out of Benjamin's door, turned left and went down the hall opposite the way to Dominic's room.

She did not react the way she was supposed to. She wasn't a mind reader.

Having followed her into the hall, he replied, "Good night," in a normal voice. Benjamin could still waken.

She said, "Sh-h-h!"

Dominic smiled down the hall at her and watched as she disappeared into her room on the other side of Benjamin's. She and her bare feet were gone from him.

Dominic slowly walked the other way and sought his own room. He undressed automatically, and he thought of all the logical reasons to justify an affair with Maria's daughter. He thought of ways in which he might try to placate Maria's resulting high indignation. Disgusted with himself, he then brushed his teeth and went to bed.

Women complicated a man's simple life. Without them, life would be so easy.

His big hands moved, kneading his pillow, then he put it under his head and sighed. Women were a distraction.

Three

—

Dominic woke at dawn. He needed little sleep. He was programmed to do as his mind directed. He got up and went to the window. Naked, he stood there and looked out on fog. It had crept in from the warm lake to meet the cool air. It wisped through the trees and hung in softening veils.

Vision was limited. The fog made everything mysterious. From such concealment, knights could ride out to the rescue of fair maidens...who were brunette with blue-green eyes. The knights would be wearing armor that creaked, and they would be riding powerful breath-chuffing horses, with the thuds of the heavy hooves muted by the sound-capturing fog.

Life wasn't like that. It was more grim. Loveless. Spineless—disappointing.

Dominic sighed and left the window to pull on jogging clothes, socks and running shoes. He stood up and stretched, moving, bending. He opened a small cabinet refrigerator and took out orange juice that he drank from the carton.

Continuing to move his arms and body, to stretch his legs as he warmed up, he walked down the stairs quietly and nodded to the prowling shadow guards. Dominic punched buttons so that no alarm would go off; then he went silently out into the magic morning.

He ran. His track had a set pattern, so that none of his men would be surprised. The course went back and forth through the trees within the compound, then down to the sandy beach.

It was exhilarating to run. He had still been a young man when he had begun, and it had lifted his life. Running, he felt free.

In the foggy morning, the birds were quiet. Against the muted sound of traffic, there was only the whispering sound of his shoes on the grass and the different sound his stride made in the dirt of the lane as he crossed it. His breath was easy. He felt alive.

Returning to the house, he removed his fog-wet, lane-dirtied shoes and went stocking-footed up the stairs. His breathing was still deep and sweat filmed his body. His suit was wet across his back, around his waist and under his arms.

When he reached the top of the stairs, his glance instantly went to her door. *Her* door? It was his house. But he stopped. His body remembered her lying asleep in his chair, lax, soft, inviting. He moved slowly down the hallway toward the closed portal, drawn to her.

"Good morning." The Italian words came from his child.

Startled, Dominic jerked his head around and saw through the open door that Benjamin was sitting on the floor of his own room with all his small-child Lego pieces scattered around him. His voice quiet, Dominic asked in Italian, "What are you doing up at this time?"

"You are up."

Going into the room, Dominic smiled at his son, mentally shaking his head as to the clashes of wills coming in twelve years with Benjamin at fifteen. He squatted down and said, "Where is...Fiona?"

"I went in—" he gestured to the connecting door that stood open "—but she still sleeps."

Dominic's glance shot toward the open door. Riveted, his toned muscles allowed him to rise slowly to his feet. Casually he mentioned, "She could be up. I will see." And he went to the doorway to look in on Fiona.

Her hair was an artful shadow on her pillow. She lay curled under the light blanket in the morning chill. It would be very easy for him to step into her room, close and lock the connecting door and go over to her bed.

"See?" Benjamin's head was down below Dominic's hip. Benjamin pointed to the bed. "She sleeps."

"You had her up last night." The words weren't really even chiding.

Benjamin turned up his face so that he could see the great distance to his father's eyes. "Night is...*dif-fir-unt*."

Dominic looked at his son. He, too, might hear knights in the fog. He replied, "Yes."

On the bed, Fiona stirred with the puzzling sound of male voices. She yawned and stretched, her bare arms reaching up out from under the blanket. Dominic got to see that before he realized that Benjamin was going toward the bed. "No!" he rasped in a harsh whisper.

Benjamin was startled, but he came back to his father with curiosity. He whispered in the strident way of children. "Why not?"

"Benjamin?" Her voice came from the bed.

"You are up!" Benjamin's voice was joyous as he turned back toward her.

Slowly, still stretching, she half sat up. "Almost." She smiled over at the child who stood alone in the doorway.

"See, Papa? She is up!" He turned to look up, then turned more and looked behind him, then went into the other room questioning, "Papa?"

Papa? Fiona's eyes widened and she lay back as she quickly pulled the blanket up to her nose.

Benjamin came back into her room. "He went away."

"He was here?" She questioned in Italian.

"Yes. But he went away. Are you awake?"

In English, she replied, "Mostly." Dominic would not have been in her room. Benjamin just meant that his father had been in his room. That was all. She lowered the blanket to her chin. "Are you wide-awake?"

Benjamin grinned. "Yes." And he sighed hugely as the adults did when he was off-schedule. Adults were peculiar about time.

She mentioned, "It's only six-thirty."

He replied, in English, "My tummy's hungry."

"Your clock is fouled up."

"My clock?"

She explained, "The one that wakes you and makes you eat and sleep."

"Where is it?"

"Inside your head, I think. Come here. Let me see if I can hear it ticking."

Benjamin climbed up on her bed and nestled down beside her. She put the blanket over him, too, and they were quiet. After a time he wriggled, but she said, "Sh-h-h, I'm listening."

And he went to sleep.

Showered and dressed, Dominic Lorenzo came cautiously back to his son's door. There was no sound. He ventured quietly into the room and over to the open connecting door. Carefully, he looked inside, then moved to stand in the door. His son was asleep in her arms. That lucky child. She, too, slept.

He stood watching for some time, then he moved softly from the door to cross Benjamin's room and go out into the hall. He went down the stairs, out the door to his anonymously silver car, and drove from the compound.

Upstairs, her eyes now open, Fiona listened as he drove away. What had he seen as he had stood all that time in Benjamin's doorway? Why had he waited there? Had he come back to tell Benjamin goodbye? Dominic probably did not approve of her putting the child into her bed. He'd be a Spartan. At age six, his child would be taken from his mother and started in training as a warrior.

She lay, thinking of her arguments and defiances of such orders from that silent and smoldering man. And he would look at her, and he could come to her—and she'd better think of something else.

Fiona was plotting out the day of activities that would allow Benjamin to sleep all through the next night. He would have no nap. They would be on their feet at all times, except when they ate. He would go to bed at six that evening and sleep until eight the next day. Right.

Of course, she was leaving that evening. But the night sitter would have a pleasant rest. She would read.... It was so snuggly under that blanket with the child warm and curled beside her. She thought about what book they could read that day. And Fiona went to sleep.

It was after nine when they wakened. They hurried around and dressed. They went downstairs to an enormous breakfast. Fiona said, in English, to Momma, "Why on earth didn't you waken us?"

Momma raised her brows and shook her head, making the earrings bounce as she replied toploftily in Italian, "You are to speak our language."

"You understood." Fiona used English.

"Benjamin is to learn the language." Momma was positive in Italian.

Fiona continued, in English, "He knows it."

"He understands some of the words, and he uses simple ones," Momma directed in Italian. "He must become proficient."

"He needs English to speak in the schools." Speaking that language, Fiona raised tit-for-tat eyebrows.

"I shall speak to Lorenzo about this," Momma said in her tongue.

In her own, Fiona replied, "Good. I am leaving this afternoon. I shall not be back until in the morning. There must be someone here with Benjamin tonight."

Momma eyed her. In English, she inquired distastefully, "You are courting?"

"No." Fiona used snippy Italian. "I am employed. I need my job secure. I must go there and keep in touch with what is happening."

Momma smiled. "I shall contact Lorenzo."

"Do that."

Benjamin had two naps that day. He went to sleep during lunch, slumped back in his chair, out cold. Fiona tried to talk him awake and then to jostle him awake, but he was dead-asleep, his body waggling like a rag doll's.

In Italian, Momma scolded Fiona for exhausting the child.

Fiona sassed back in English and requested her car. Instead, she was driven by Nick to see her mother. They rode in that cumbersome black car, but did not fall through any bridges or overpasses, so it probably was not as heavy as it looked.

At the hospital, Nick parked in the same no-parking zone and waved off Fiona's protests. He escorted her to her mother's floor. Various relatives greeted Fiona and murmurs were exchanged before the nurse was there to smile at Nick and take Fiona in to see her mother.

Tomas greeted Fiona. "Your father went home to sleep a while. He is fine."

"Thank you," she replied automatically in Italian. They walked along, leaving Nick in the waiting room. Tomas seemed not to even notice the nurse. When Fiona went into her mother's room, Tomas stood outside the door and waited.

The nurse said to Fiona, "She has been awake, but it's been only twenty-four hours. We might get her up tomorrow, but we definitely will the next day."

"Already?"

"Oh, yes. She'll have physical therapy for several days before she goes home."

"When will that be?" Fiona was amazed.

"A week or so. We'll see how she gets along. She'll be in therapy for a while after she's home. She'll probably have a walker or crutches, at first."

"That seems quite fast." Fiona was doubtful.

"She'll be ready," the nurse replied. "She's a fighter."

"That is true." Fiona looked at her sleeping mother. She looked so... fragile.

The nurse asked Fiona, "Is he married?"

Fiona had to blink and realign her thoughts. The nurse was speaking of Tomas. "I don't think so."

"Is he going with anyone?"

"I'll find out."

The nurse cautioned, "Be subtle. Don't let him think I asked."

"Never." Fiona gave the nurse a disgruntled look. Why would she want to get tangled up with any male Italian?

Fiona turned again to her sleeping mother. Her brain's time clock would be as screwed up as Benjamin's. Hospitals didn't recognize time was divided. They did things around the clock. The only difference was that they dimmed the lights at night.

The nurse went out into the hall, and Fiona heard her animated chatter near the door. She was flirting with Tomas. What about her other patients? She was zonked by Tomas. Shame on her. What was it about Italian men that women found so alluring? Only half-Italian, Fiona could not fathom it.

She sat there watching her frail-looking mother sleep. Her mother had never appeared subject to time or mortality, and to see her looking frail unsettled Fiona. She couldn't say that to her father. Or her siblings. Who could she talk to about mortality who wouldn't then become aware of time?

She looked at the flowers, and especially noted one enormous bouquet. It would be from her father. She went over and smiled as she looked at the card. But the signature read, "Dominic." He had sent those flowers. He should have. He was respon—no, he was not. It had been her careless, lighthearted mother's stupidity. Fiona glared at her drug-sedated mother, irritated with her for being hurt and making her daughter feel insecure.

Fiona said to the sleeping woman, "He stood in the door and watched us sleeping in bed. I wasn't sleeping, of course, but Benjamin was and..."

Her mother's lips moved. "Take care of Benjam—"

Good grief, *that* again? What about her? What about Maria Garibaldi Evans's daughter, Fiona? "He has my car, you know. The guts are out of it, and I can't get the car back. I'll probably find it's been sold over into Canada!"

Her mother moved her lips as if to smile? Or was she thirsty?

Fiona went to the door and interrupted the nurse, who went on talking as if Fiona were not standing right there. Fiona said, "Pardon me—"

To give a free path for Fiona to leave, the nurse moved closer to Tomas. Tomas didn't back away.

Fiona asked, "Shall I give my mother some water? Is it all right if she has some? She seems dehydrated."

The nurse smiled at Fiona and said, "She just drank a full glass—" she consulted her watch, turning her wrist so that her forearm brushed Tomas's chest "—about forty-two minutes ago. Give her some if you want to."

Fiona stepped back, closed the door and stalked over to the bed. She lifted the glass and looked at her mother, and she felt great tears well from her eyes. Very gently she said, "Oh, Mom—" And with exquisite tenderness she said, "Here, do you want some water?"

With the straw put to the corner of her mouth, her mother took an automatic sip or two, then turned her head away. She had had enough.

Fiona went on, "He walks like a panther, you know. You've seen him. Did you notice that?"

Her mother's mouth had relaxed and she bubbled a tiny snore.

Fiona went back to sit in the chair. She felt as if she were all alone in the world, that there was no one on whom she could depend. Look at her Gibraltar mother, flat out, injured, in bed and out cold.

When her time was up Fiona went to the door, and the nurse said, "I'll tell her that you sat with her today."

"Thank you."

Tomas told her, in Italian. "I, too, shall tell her. I will give your love to her. And I will tell your father that you were here and asked after him."

"Yes." Fiona felt unneeded.

Tomas said, "The nurse takes care only of your mother."

"Is that necessary?"

"It is the way it should be," Tomas assured her. Then he elaborated. "There are three nurses."

"Oh." She felt a little scared that it would cost that much. "Does Mother have insurance, working with Benjamin?"

"She has Lorenzo."

What did that mean?

They walked back to the waiting room, Tomas was exchanged for Nick and Nick took Fiona out to the black car. Another cop waited patiently. Nick put Fiona into the car, then he nodded to the patrolman, handed over his driver's license and took the ticket.

Fiona did not say anything until they left the hospital grounds, then she directed Nick to take her downtown to her office. He did not give her any argument, but he did radio in and tell someone where they were going.

At her office building, Nick parked in front, got out and almost missed helping Fiona out of the car. He chided her, "A lady waits."

"How chauvinistic."

"Women are precious and need care."

Maybe she could understand the lure of Italian men, after all. She did need some care, right then. Fiona walked into the building and took the elevator to her office.

There, everyone was busy. She had never realized how *busy* they were! She stood until someone glanced up and said, "Fiona!" However, they went on, hurrying around.

But that triggered others, and Kevin walked out of his office with an expectant look. "Fiona?" he asked, found her with a quick look and came to her. "Are you okay?"

This was America. People spoke English. "I'm okay. Are you getting along all right?"

"Oh, yes. Angelina has been great. She pitched right in. She's taking care of things for you. I'm glad you had her in mind." Then he added, "But, of course, she isn't you. Are you okay? Is there anything I can do for you?" He took her arm in gentle fingers.

She almost cried. Right there in all that normal office chaos, she just about broke down, but she rallied. "I'm having difficulty getting someone to stay the night with my mother's charge. I may have to take some more time away from work until that's settled. Is that all right with you?"

"We'll manage. I would feel better if I knew something to do for you, to help you now. I miss you."

She smiled rather waterily and said, "How sweet of you. There really isn't anything."

"Kevin!" An urgent voice called. "Telephone!"

They both looked up to realize Kevin had been paged before.

"Tell them I'll call back." Kevin was smooth.

"It's London!"

He looked at Fiona and raised his eyebrows as he grinned. "London?"

"Go ahead. I have to leave. I'll be in touch."

"Call. Each day." He walked backward as he went toward his office, and he waved before he went through the door.

"Tough about your mom," said one.

"Hey, Fiona, we've missed you!" someone said from across the room.

But everyone was busy, and she was only momentarily distracting. So she said, "Bye!"

There were some quick and some delayed responses.

And Fiona left.

Her life was like that of a pebble on a beach. Lift one out and the water of living filled in the vacant space, then moved the other stones until her space was filled. She was not really needed.

She went down to the car rather pensively. Her big blue-green eyes were sad. Nick asked, "They fire you?" His voice sounded expectant, as if he wanted her fired. He had another ticket.

"What does Lorenzo do with all the tickets you get?"

"He said to make this as convenient as possible for you."

She tightened her mouth. "I can walk from a parking lot."

"Benjamin needs you," Nick said that with such sweetness.

Did he realize she was not feeling needed? She allowed him to tuck her into the clumsy automobile. And Nick drove her back to the compound.

Momma had vanished. Romano loomed and said, "You must stay."

"Look. I have a life. I have to get back to it. You find someone else to be with Benjamin."

"We are searching." Romano was grave.

Fiona waved her hands. "Who stayed with Benjamin when my mother had the flu?"

"Momma."

"Then, why can't she do that now?"

"She says no." Romano was patient. "She is busy."

Fiona said through her teeth, "*So am I!* I need to speak to Lorenzo."

Romano agreed. "I will see what I can do about that."

Insincerely, she commented, "How kind."

The shifts met in the kitchen for supper. The men ate greedily of the succulent foods Momma had prepared and left for them. They teased Benjamin and cast quick looks at Fiona.

She saw that Benjamin liked being with the men. Why could they not take care of him? "Why can't one of you stay the night with Benjamin?"

Romano looked surprised she'd mention that. "It isn't done."

"Someone has watched him while I was gone. Who was that?"

They shifted in their chairs. Romano explained, "We have an emergency plan. One of us is with him all the time. We switch. But it leaves us short a man each time."

"Why do you guard so closely?" she asked. "What is the danger?"

"Robbers." Romano gestured. "Kidnappers."

"I really cannot understand all this." Fiona was a little cross. "I came just yesterday to fill in for my mother, and you must have someone who can substitute for her. Find someone."

"You do not care about Benjamin?" one of the younger men inquired.

Fiona looked down at the little boy who was watching her with interest. She became intensely aware of what they had been saying in front of him. "Of course, I care about him," she said stoutly.

Romano declared logically, "Then there is no problem."

"I am not his mother. I am no kin to him. I have obligations. I can be here during the day, but I need to go to my own place. Do you understand?"

Romano pronounced, "I will try to contact Lorenzo."

"You have said that before. Do it."

Dominic Lorenzo didn't call back or come to the compound.

Fiona put Benjamin to bed rather late. But they were up during the night. He had slept too long the afternoon the day before, while she was at the hospital.

Dominic came up onto the porch and opened the door to hear Benjamin laughing. He smiled and, following the sound, he tracked them to the kitchen. Again he stood in the shadows of the hall to watch.

Benjamin was bright-eyed and alert. Fiona was sleepy-eyed and a little mussed. Her hair was in disarray around her shoulders, and her wrapper was loose. She was sleepy. She looked the way a man wanted a woman to look at night. Dominic's hot gaze went over her.

Romano had said Fiona wanted to go back to her own place each night. Dominic knew that he should let her. It was dangerous for her to be there where he could see her. Just looking at her made his desire concentrate painfully. She made him ache.

For his own sake, he should let her be. How could he do that, when it was such exquisite torture to see her? Look at her. Watch her.

Fiona had a bow that she was using to tell the old story of the villain, the heroine and the hero. The villain demanded rent money, the heroine said she could not pay and the hero said he would. She differentiated the characters by moving the bow from a mustache to a hair bow to a bow tie. Benjamin thought that was funny, especially when Fiona altered her voice for each character. It didn't take much to entertain a child.

When the story was finished and they'd laughed nicely, Dominic clapped and said, "Brava!" as he walked into the kitchen.

She grabbed her robe together at her throat and was tongue-tied. Benjamin said, in English, "It's Papa!" He looked the long way up to his father's distracted face. "Come," he told his father. "Fiona will give you cocoa."

Dominic looked at her. "Will you?" He used English.

Benjamin coached, "You say 'please.'"

Looking at her very solemnly, Dominic said softly, "Please."

She rose and turned her back. Walking to the stove, she quickly rearranged her robe more modestly and tied the sash tightly. She found a cup and saucer, then poured a cup of steaming cocoa. She carried it back and put it on the other side of Benjamin from where she was sitting.

Still standing, Dominic picked up the cup and tasted the brew. "Ahh," he said, still in English. "It has been some time since I had cocoa."

She said tautly, "I must speak to you."

He nodded. "So I heard. My son exhausts you?"

"No. But I need to go home at night. I have to keep up with my own life."

"Your job?"

"Not this week," she admitted. "I found a substitute—a brief one, of course. I can fill in until you find someone during the day for Benjamin. I can stay a week. But my job could be in jeopardy if it was longer than that."

"You could be hired here," he suggested. "It will be some time before Maria can return to us."

"I like my job," she countered.

He switched to Italian. "Then we will see what we can do. We do appreciate the compassionate way that you came to us so quickly. This is so, eh, Benjamin?"

The talk had lulled the boy.

Sticking to English, Fiona said, "Drink your cocoa, Benjamin. Perhaps when it's all gone, your papa will carry you upstairs." She looked across the boy to Dominic. He was watching her with that smoldering look. The impact of him went down into her body in the scariest way. She needed to get out of that house.

He watched her cheeks flush a little and he bit his lower lip. She was a peach ripe for the plucking.

And yet again he reminded himself, she was Maria Garibaldi's daughter. But he thought of the women he had had. Each had been some woman's daughter. So? How was this one different?

He watched Fiona as she helped Benjamin finish his cocoa. Her lips parted as his son drank from the cup. Dominic was mesmerized as her tongue peeked out for a quick lick as Benjamin's tongue cleaned his small mouth. And the man waited for the woman to look at him again.

She sent a quick glance to him and her cheeks became darker with her self-consciousness. She said to Benjamin, "There. Now ask your papa if he will take you up to bed."

Dominic thought, Why don't you ask me that, Fiona?

Benjamin said, "Now, Papa?"

Still looking at Fiona, Dominic said, "Now."

Four

————

Dominic stayed away from his house all of the next day. He was aware that he stayed away. Then he was struck with the fact that he had *never* gone home during the day! How could he figure he was "staying away"? That did not make sense.

But he thought only of Fiona. The Lorenzo building was near the Tribune building along the Chicago River. From his window, Dominic could look down either way along the river or he could look out between the buildings and see Lake Michigan.

He lay back in his desk chair and looked out at the lake, blue under the early September sky, and he would see her eyes. Her eyes were not that blue, they were blue-green.

There was a streak of water over there that was exactly the blue-green of her eyes. Wasn't it? He would have to see her eyes again. Tonight he would go into her room, get into her bed, kiss her awake and look into her eyes to see if they were the color of that streak in Lake Michigan.

Dominic frowned out of his window, worried about what was happening to him. He was not old enough for a mid-life crisis, was he? He did not need to be this involved with any woman.

His first wife had been a witch. He had not known she had been pregnant twice and had aborted the babies. Then he found they probably had not been his. He had been young, then, just building his empire. But she had soured him on relationships. Sex had become a function after that.

Then there had been Tate. Tate Lambert of Texas. She had come into his life like a comet. She had been so alive and vibrant that she had distracted him from business for too long.

When Tate had said she was pregnant, Dominic had been astonished. And suspicious. After his experience with his first wife, he had wondered if the child could be his. He had had the test run, which had removed all doubt, and he had married her. So, he had had a son. He swore he would build the greatest power base in the world for his son. And he had worked hard to do that.

He had never needed much sleep. He found the puzzles and challenges and plotting of the ramifications of his agri-business fulfilling. And sometimes he had even forgotten that he had a wife. He would go home, his mind immersed in strategy, and for a split second he would be startled to see a woman in his bed.

He still could not understand why Tate had divorced him. Women were baffling. But he had his son. He no longer needed a permanent woman. They were, at best, a distraction, and, at worst, they were pure hell. His first wife had been hell; Tate had been a distraction until he had controlled his reaction to her. It was best not to be involved.

Why was he so fascinated with Fiona Evans? Besides being really beautiful, she was exactly like any other woman. The only thing wrong about her was that she did not appear to be the kind of woman who would allow him to satisfy his need of her so that he could forget her.

And she didn't give any of the signals women gave men to approach them. She was interested, at least her body was, but her mind rejected him. She would be a challenge. But if he breached her defenses and took her, what would that do to her?

For the first time, Dominic considered what his interference might do to another person. He'd always known what needed doing, and he'd done it. But he couldn't seduce Fiona. He suspected that, if they came together, it would not be an ordinary mating. She... and maybe even he...would never be the same again.

Romano said she had a temper, this Fiona. That she was furious to find her car gone. Why should that bother her? It had needed some work. He was having it done for her. Why had that made her angry?

Women liked that kind of attention. They liked having a man who spent money on them. He had been doing her a favor for taking over Maria's job—and here she had become angry about the whole thing.

But then he had seen her and been riveted by her. He had been unprepared, because he had never glimpsed even a picture of her. But now that he had seen her, he wanted to just stare at her. No, he wanted to see more of her. All of her.

Soberly, Dominic stood up and went over to the window to lean against the frame and look down at the river below him. Her office was not far from his. He had gone over to look at Kevin McBride. This was the man whom Tomas said had gone to the hospital, hoping that Fiona was there. McBride had turned his back on Tomas and tried to talk privately with Ned Evans. Tomas had reported that with some glee.

So Dominic had gone over to Fiona's office and glanced inside. There he had evaluated the man Tomas had described and smiled a little.

McBride was no threat. No deterrent. He was not the man for Fiona.

Just thinking that sobered Dominic. He was staking a claim on Fiona? He was territorial about her? And he admitted it. He was going to know her. He was going to taste her honey and revel in her body. He was going to have her.

His body agreed.

And he would be kind. When they parted, he would set her up in a business of her own. When he was satisfied and bored again, he would do that very kindly. This time it would be he who severed the relationship.

So he went home when he knew that Benjamin would be napping. She would be there, alone, and there would be no interruptions. How did a man start a conversation with a wary woman?

As he drove the silver car toward his compound, he tried to remember if he had ever before met a wary, reluctant, resisting woman. Other than the comet who had been Tate, he remembered only bold and brassy ones. Women who put their hands on him and whispered shockingly salacious invitations into his ear and tickled his palm as they slipped notes into his hand.

Why couldn't Fiona do that? It would save a lot of his time.

Was she a tease? Had her mother put her up to this? Why had she come there so quickly? Maria was barely in the hospital before Fiona was established in his house. And she was bidding for his attention, demanding to see him all the time. About her missing car... about getting someone else to stay with Benjamin...

That didn't seem as if she was trying for him. That sounded as if she were trying to get away. She was threatening the men with leaving Benjamin alone with just them.

Dominic smiled. All those big, hard men were stopped dead in their tracks to think of taking care of one little boy. What could be so difficult about a little child less than half their size?

He pulled up by the house and saw her car had been returned. That made him frown. How could he keep her caged there, if she had a car? Had Romano given her back her keys? Probably. What excuse could he have for not letting her have them?

With Dominic Lorenzo emerging from his car, Romano came to him.

Dominic lifted his chin to indicate Fiona's car. "So you brought it back. Have you given her the keys?" And he gave his loyal friend a cold look.

"Yes." Then he shrugged and shook his head once. "She has not yet tried to start it." He smiled a little.

"It does not start?"

"Somehow." He put his hands out from his body in a helpless manner.

Dominic slapped Romano's shoulder. "Good."

Romano said, "Benjamin and Fiona are down at the lakefront."

Dominic nodded slowly. So. Benjamin was not napping. That annoyed Dominic. How could he court a woman with a kid underfoot? There had to be ways.

So Dominic went up to his room and changed into swim trunks and a soft pullover that showed he was entirely male. No question.

He left his room, went back downstairs, exited the house and went down to the lake beach. Each year, he paid a small fortune to keep the shoreline in grainy sand. The current was wrong along the lakefront there, and the sand would erode with the big storms.

To see Fiona playing along the beach was worth coming back to the compound, and every penny he had paid for sand had been well spent. Dominic didn't even see Benjamin.

Fiona had on a halter top and short shorts. Dominic could not have told the colors because he saw only her tousled hair and her skin. She ran, laughing, and her breasts bounced. He saw that.

She saw him and stopped. Benjamin ran and "caught" her around her knees, making her stagger. She put her hands down on him to keep him from falling, and Dominic was impressed with her balance. She kept her cautious stare on him.

He grinned at her, slouching a little, conscious of his movements, exaggerating them a little. He realized he wanted her to see him as a man. A physical male.

Benjamin then turned and saw him. "It's Papa," he told Fiona.

Dominic looked at his son a little sourly. Why couldn't he be napping?

Fiona took Benjamin's hand, and they started toward Dominic.

She was coming to meet him.

As she approached, she said, "My car was returned to me. What were the costs of the repairs?"

Of all the greetings she could have made, he had not thought of that one. No smiles of thanks. Only the sour fact that the car had been *returned,* and her demand for the bill.

He considered her. Was she worth the trouble she was going to take? His gaze dropped down her clinging lake-splashed clothing. She looked nearly nude. He glanced at her long legs and small feet. He looked into her blue-green eyes and then out over the lake to see if he could compare them to that streak of color. But he was distracted by her nearness and he sighed.

Using English as a courteous concession to her, he said, "Hello, Benjamin."

"May I splash you?" He bent down and cupped his hands in the water, looking up at his father, his eyes glinting with mischief.

Dominic had to laugh. Staying with English, he warned, "Not unless you want to get dunked."

The snippy woman intruded. "I would like the bill for my car repairs."

She could be a real pain. "I don't have it on me."

"How can I get a copy?" Fiona asked prissily.

With some irony, Dominic replied, "I'll have Romano make one out."

".I would appreciate that." She tightened her lips and lifted her chin. "Have you found someone for Benjamin for the evenings?"

"We're working on it." He had begun to feel gloomy, but then he noticed that she was taking little peeks at him. She tilted her head a lot, and as she did she looked around, and in the many dartings of her gaze she looked at his face, but once he caught her looking at his body. She looked at Dominic Lorenzo. He could not prevent a slight smile, but he did not laugh out loud. Fortunately.

Still courteously using her language, he told her, "Your mother was up for a while today."

Her face became vulnerable. "Did you stop in to see her?"

That surprised him. "Uh . . . no."

"Oh."

"I . . . should have." He ventured that.

"Mother would have been so pleased . . . if you had." She looked up with the last three words. They were an indictment. He had not thought to go to see Maria.

He switched to Italian. "I do not remember that it is important to other people."

That seemed such a strange statement. He did not say "people" but "other people." He considered himself as separate from everyone else? Her tongue followed into his language. "You do not like people to come to see you?"

"I am never here." He gestured to the grounds.

"Have you no friends?"

"Many." He turned to walk along the beach, and since Benjamin took his hand, Fiona followed absently and he adjusted his steps so that she walked along with them. He walked in the water, Benjamin was in the spending waves, and she walked on the wet sand. She was curious and therefore not conscious that he was leading her to do as he wished. He said, "The people I choose to know, I meet in business."

"But not at other times?"

He glanced at her. "There's no need."

"What do you do on the holidays?"

"Catch up on the backlog of work that can be put aside."

"You don't celebrate any of the holidays?" She did not believe that.

"Momma decorates the house and makes big meals. The men eat too much and are groggy. I have to patrol to be sure they aren't sleeping."

"Is there really danger here? Do you really need the patrols and guards?"

He shrugged. "I have never tested that. I have patrols and guards." He looked around. "In another two months, we will move to the winter place. You will like it. It is Italian. Snug for winter. A marble jewel."

"I would think this place would be beautiful in winter, with the fireplaces and the trees all bare and the lake waves high. I would think you would want to stay here."

"In winter, this house is a drafty barn."

"And the . . . Italian place?"

"Would you like to go look at it? It cost a mint." Was he bragging on his money? Was he trying to impress her? Yes. He was a fool. No sane man who wanted a woman would tell her he was worth so much. She would dig her greedy claws in deeper.

He glanced over at Fiona. He would love to have her touch him in any way at all, and if it pleased her to only dig her claws into him, he wanted that . . . at least for a time. Long enough. He looked at her. He wanted her.

It felt very nice to walk along the costly sandy beach with his son and a woman whom he desired. It felt natural. That was an interesting thought for him.

When had he wanted to be with a woman outside of his bed? Tate, for a while. His gaze came back to Fiona. She was different from any woman he had ever known.

Benjamin loved her.

He observed his son chattering to Fiona. The child was comfortable with her. She touched him gently. She smiled at the boy. Why didn't she smile at the man in that way?

Disregarding his son's story, Dominic interrupted, "Do you wish to go and see your mother today?"

"I have my car."

Dominic had to lower his eyelashes over his eyes to conceal the fact that he knew her car would not start. "Yes." Then he said, with a quiet apology that was cleverly done, "We still have no one to stay tonight with Benjamin. Could you? Just one more night."

With great exasperation she took a deep breath and let it out rather impatiently, as she looked off to the side. She said, "One more, and that's all. Do you understand that?"

He had watched her chest as she took that breath. He now replied silkily, "Perfectly." His voice was slow and gentle and his smile was like a Cheshire cat's.

She looked up quickly at his silky tone, but he was looking down at his son. So she thought she had misinterpreted him. His expression was so benign that she thought how he must love his child.

He barely knew Benjamin. The boy recognized his father, but there was no great excitement in Benjamin when Dominic Lorenzo appeared. He did not run to Dominic. The boy was simply a welcoming, friendly child. He greeted Romano with greater enthusiasm.

Dominic then realized that if he was going to lure
Fiona into his net, his bait would be the boy. She
stayed there for Benjamin. Even then, she wiggled on
the hook. Dominic would have to ensnare her; and to
catch her attention, he would have to use the boy.
Therefore, he would have to be around and learn how
to court a woman with a child as witness.

He took off the pullover and gave it to Benjamin
before he walked into the deeper water to cool off. He
swam a way, and Benjamin stood in the small, break-
ing waves and watched. Fiona rescued the pullover and
carried it in her hand. It was still warm from his body.

As Dominic paralleled the shoreline, Benjamin ran
along, waving his arms, scaring the birds and yelling.

To be sure that the child did not veer into the water, Fiona had to keep up, so she jogged along. Dominic's strokes slowed so that he could watch her
jogging. He started just on the movement of her hips
and breasts, but her face captured him. She laughed at
Benjamin and her hand gathered her hair, to control
it from the playful wind.

Ah, to be that wind, curling around her body, teasing her wet shorts and peaking her nipples beneath the
water-splashed top before tousling her hair. He swam
a little farther.

Benjamin could not keep up and stopped to watch
after his father. Fiona took his hand. "We'll meet him
up the beach."

"I swim slow." He used English.

"Slowly." Fiona corrected.

"Yes."

"He's bigger. When you're that big, you'll swim the
way he swims."

Benjamin smiled. "Yes." Then he reached up his arms. "Tired. Carry Benjamin."

When he began to abbreviate his sentences, he was really tired.

Fiona lifted him into her arms. He weighed a ton. "Do you have rocks in your pockets?"

She always asked that. He said "No-o-o," but he put his head on her shoulder and looked from under her chin.

Dominic saw her lift the boy, and he headed for shore. He could run faster than he could swim in the current.

He came to them, stripping water off his body. His hair was dripping. "Here. Let me carry him."

"You're wet."

"So is he." Dominic began to take the boy from her, his water-cold hands touching her heat, touching her.

"I'll get a towel." She put Benjamin down. "It's just back a way. Then you can dry off a little."

He walked along, holding Benjamin's hand. He said to the boy, "You cannot be a sleepyhead."

"No." His steps lagged.

"When you go to sleep, you quit all at once," Dominic observed.

"Yes."

Fiona came back with the towel, handing it to Dominic. Then she stood mesmerized as he dried his hair and wiped down his body. She would like to have done that for him.

He saw that. "Did I get dry enough?"

She nodded little nods.

In English, he said, "Okay, Benjamin, you get to ride."

He picked up the boy effortlessly. Benjamin told
Fiona, "See? He doesn't think I have rocks."

"Rocks?" Dominic looked over at Fiona, glad for
the excuse.

"He's heavy. I accuse him of carrying rocks."

Dominic staggered. "It *is* rocks. I thought swimming so vigorously had weakened me!" And with the
words, he stumbled and said to Fiona, "Help me. He's
too heavy."

Benjamin laughed that delicious way of children
who are truly amused. He shifted and said to Fiona,
"Help Papa. I'm too heavy."

And without thinking, Fiona put her arms around
Benjamin . . . and Dominic. She laughed up at Benjamin, whose new perch had given him better height.
"Two of us," she complained. "It takes *two* of us to
carry this bag of heavy rocks!" But then she realized
what she was doing, and that her arms were mostly
around Dominic, and that his arm was between her
breasts. She abruptly let go and stepped back.

Dominic knew exactly what had happened, but he
was smart enough to immediately falter.

Benjamin was involved. "Help Papa! I'm too
heavy! He'll fall!"

"Pick a soft place," she said flippantly. But her
cheeks were scarlet and she kept her distance.

So Dominic staggered around. "Is that soft
enough?" he would ask Benjamin.

"No, no!" exclaimed Benjamin. He was wakening
with the excitement of the silly game and enjoying the
drama.

Fiona was carrying the towel. She dropped Dominic's pullover so that she could spread the towel down
on some sand, as she asked, "How is that?"

Benjamin put his little hands on his father's face and turned it as he pointed to the towel and asked, "There?"

Dominic agreed. "Let's try it."

He eased down, then sprawled at the last minute, deliberately tumbling Benjamin with clever care.

Benjamin said, "We found a place!"

Dominic looked up at Fiona and said, "Yes."

"Come down, Fiona!" Benjamin was laughing as he patted the little strip of towel left over.

"We have to move over to give her some room." Dominic put Benjamin on his lap, then, as swift as a striking snake, his arm reached out for Fiona.

She did not want to sit on that excessively shrinking beach towel with that potent man. She laughed, but she also seriously twisted her wrist, trying to free herself from his iron grasp. It was hopeless, and she was slowly drawn down. He did that one-handed.

She wondered why women ever believe they have control over their circumstances? They should be careful. They are no physical match for men. She was no physical match for Dominic. She was...well, in a way...

Benjamin reached over and hugged Fiona's head to him. He then confided to his father, "I love Fiona."

"You have good taste." Dominic's smoldering eyes looked at his victim.

Fiona said, "Let go, or I'll clobber your chops."

Benjamin had to fall back laughing. "Clobber your slobber!"

"Sorry." Dominic took her arm in his other hand and rubbed the red mark left by his own hand. "You are so fair for a brunette. My fingerprints will show on your skin."

"Let go."

"Why?" Dominic's smile was as dangerous to a susceptible woman as a tiger's to a bleating lamb.

"I don't want your fingerprints on me."

His voice was low and as sexy as all sin. "Are there someone elses?" And he looked down her, as if searching for the evidence that some other man had claimed her.

"No."

"What about Kevin McBride?" Dominic's confident eyes were lazy and smoky dark.

She didn't ask why Dominic would know Kevin's name. "He's my boss."

"No involvement?" Dominic made the query careless.

"Of course not."

"'Of course—not'? He's nice enough looking. Why not?"

"I'm a businesswoman."

The chuckle in Dominic's throat would have lured out a woman who was hopelessly stuck in a tar pit.

Benjamin had left them, they had not even noticed that. He came back with Fiona's shirt. "You shivered. You cold? Here."

"Thank you." She took the shirt.

"You shivered?" Dominic asked. "Why?"

She refused to reply. She got up from the towel as he watched avidly, his forearms resting on his bent-up knees. She shook out the shirt and put it on. It was enormous and swallowed her.

"Whose shirt is that?"

Separated from him, she said quite aloofly, "Mine."

"Whose was it?" And dangerous undertones laced the simple words, surprising him considerably.

"Marshall Field's." She said the two words with élan.

"I trust you do mean the department store?" His voice grated.

She smiled just a little.

He rose to his knees in a prowling way.

"My life, and what I do in it, is no concern of yours." She turned away. "Come, Benjamin, you need a shower and dry clothing." She started away.

"You forgot the towel." Dominic rose and shook it out.

"You used it last. It's yours. You take it back." And off she marched, followed by Benjamin who skipped along, keeping up.

Dominic watched her leave him and he smiled after her. Benjamin turned and waved, and Dominic noticed in time to lift his hand and wave back. Fiona did not turn around.

Dominic shook out the towel and folded it nicely. He went back to where his abandoned top lay and shook the sand from it, too. He pulled it on and then ran up and down the beach getting rid of energy, or maybe it was frustration.

She was a pain. A sweet, thrillingly uncomfortable pain. He was going to get her. He was going to get her into his bed and make a feast of her, and she was going to love every nuance. She was going to purr and move and gasp and clutch at him.

He was still running back and forth when Nick came down to the beach and waited, signaling Dominic to stop.

"What?" Dominic's face was blank as he waited the two seconds for a reply.

"She is angrier than a witch. Her car would not start, so she took the small car. You know it is not automatic, so she ran it into a tree, got out and is walking to the gate. She is getting away."

And Dominic laughed.

Five

"**B**e quick!" commanded Dominic of Nick. "Run back and get Benjamin. Meet us at the gate. Hurry!"

They separated, running in different directions—flat-out, serious running. Since Fiona was walking, Dominic was already at the gate and his breathing was back to normal.

He looked barbaric, like one of the Romans who had stolen the Sabine women. Fiona's firm steps faltered as she lifted her chin. A contradiction, there.

With indolence, Dominic had the guts to inquire, in Italian, "Walking?"

That *infuriated* Fiona, and she spent precious seconds gasping in air as she searched for a withering retort.

And Nick arrived on a motorbike with Benjamin—in the "nick" of time.

Dominic Lorenzo smiled.

Benjamin's schedule had not been at all regular. He badly needed a nap. He had been delayed twice already, and this was the third time. He was tired and cranky and being carted around, when all he wanted was to sleep.

He saw Fiona and burst into tears, reaching out his little hand for her.

She slid a murderous look at Dominic, who was watching with concern. But he did not move, nor did he go to his child. He simply observed.

Fiona's heart was mush, anyway, where Benjamin was concerned, and a teary-eyed Benjamin was a priority. "How could you drag this child around at this time? He is exhausted! Why is he out here?"

No one said anything.

Since there wasn't anyone speaking, Benjamin said, "Fiona..."

People are people, no matter what. And a shrewd, successful businessman knows people. As Dominic had calculated, Fiona folded.

She went to Benjamin and took him from Nick. The boy wrapped his little child arms around her neck and bawled against her throat. She was dressed to go into town to see her mother, and she wore high heels. She started walking back to the house.

Nick shot a horrified glance at Dominic, who lounged against the gatepost with a satisfied expression on his face. He smiled at Nick.

Nick gestured to Fiona...walking, carrying that load of rocks named Benjamin.

Dominic shook his head and waved Nick over to the other gatepost. Then he straightened from his own post and sauntered along behind Fiona, only slowly catching up with her. He figured how far she would have to walk, carrying Benjamin, before her temper had dissipated enough that she would willingly accept help... from him.

He had underestimated her and he finally had to say "please," and after that he had to insist as he took the child. Fiona was furious. She snarled, "You are underhanded. How could you use a child this way?"

Her response irked him just a little before he was charmed that she did not realize she was his prey. She thought he only meant to have her to take care of Benjamin. So he looked astonished. "Why didn't you drive your car?" he asked in innocent Italian.

Through her teeth, she snarled, "As if you didn't know."

"What?" he asked in great puzzlement.

"It doesn't start. When I brought it here just two days ago, there was nothing wrong with it. Now the key won't even turn."

He frowned perfectly in his shock.

"You are capable of any trick to get your way," she accused. "I think you are deplorable. I have no idea why my mother respects you."

Probably because he had no desire for her mother and had always treated her with respect.

Benjamin was out cold. He was lying in his father's arms, lax, with a limp arm dangling.

When they arrived back at the house, the "small" car was still against the tree and there were two men looking into the innards of Fiona's vintage car.

In Italian, Dominic inquired, "Find the trouble?"

Romano slipped into the driver's seat and turned the key. It started.

All three men looked inquiringly at Fiona. She closed her eyes and took a deep and calming breath.

She went to the car. Romano got out, Fiona sat in the seat and turned the key—nothing happened.

She sat there, looking out into the trees and counted to one hundred.

In that time, Momma came out, scolding everyone with the sharp edge of her tongue. She took the sleeping child from Dominic, cast a censuring, stabbing glance at Fiona and marched back into the house.

Dominic joined the other two men hovering under Fiona's car hood.

She got out of the driver's seat, went over to Dominic and said, "For my mother, I will stay for these next ten days. At that time I will leave, and I shall not return. Now put the distributor back where it belongs."

She left Dominic standing there as she turned away and went into the house.

All was silent. There was the whisper of the leaves stirred by the lake breeze, the murmur of the waves lapping the expensive sand, the faint roar of distant traffic, and the birds were singing. There were no voices and all appeared peaceful.

Dominic frowned. He had "won," but he did not feel that he had been victorious. He ordered the big car brought around. No one referred to it as a limo, "big" just identified it from the "small" black car. The limo, too, was black. It was a beautiful machine.

Upstairs, with tears drying on her cheeks, Fiona was sitting at her window looking into the treetops. She turned her head at the gentle knock on her door and thought ignoring it would be too immature. She went over and opened the door. "Yes?"

The father of eleven children, Romano sucked in his breath at the sight of the dried tears. His voice very kind, he said, "Lorenzo says to—" he changed his words and as an added courtesy, he spoke then in English "—if you need to go anywhere, you could drive his car. Here are the keys."

Dominic was giving her permission to leave the compound. Being very adult about it, she replied, "I have my own car."

"It's a bucket of bolts. Lorenzo asks if you will accept his car to use. It will be safer for you."

"No." She gave him a brief nod, but she still wasn't mature enough to thank Romano. She slowly took a step back and gently closed the door, not giving him any message in reply.

Romano went to Dominic's room and knocked on the opened door. Dominic came into the room, tying his tie. "Yes?"

"She said she has her own car." Romano gave Dominic a level look. "She has been weeping."

Dominic's hands stilled for several heartbeats, then he moved a step or two and his fingers continued the motions to complete his tie knot.

Romano stood in the doorway.

Dominic went to the mirror and fiddled with the tie, then rather savagely took the knot apart to begin again. He looked toward the door in annoyance; but having seen what he wanted to know, Romano had left.

So it was that Fiona repaired her makeup to conceal the fact that she had cried, and she straightened her clothes and went down the stairs in the silent house, then out to her cleaned and washed car. She got into the driver's seat, turned the key and the motor started. She buckled her seat belt. The motor was smooth and purred like an experienced cat.

The gears shifted without the familiar hitch, and the shocks must have been replaced. It drove like a new car. Alone for the first time in several days, Fiona drove to the hospital and, as ordinary people do, she parked in the parking lot. She exited the car and walked to the entrance. There in the no-parking zone was the silver car, and standing beside it was Nick. He smiled.

She said "Stay," and walked away from him into the hospital.

Nick followed.

At the elevator, he reached first to punch the floor and, again, he smiled.

In Italian, she told him coolly, "You are a nuisance."

In English, he replied, "Yeah."

Upstairs, an obviously informed Tomas looked up immediately and watched Fiona with something like impatiently irritated respect. His lips were thinned and his jaw clenched.

Fiona greeted her father with a hug, and they spoke in English. She greeted the Evans cousin and the uncle who were there to sit with her father, and she kissed cheeks with the Garibaldis who hovered around her, speaking in Italian. They caught her up on all the hospital gossip and the fact that one of the American nurses was quite brazenly trying to lure Tomas.

"You are American." Fiona frowned.

"But we are really Italian. She is English."

"I think she's Dutch." Another put that in.

In English, Fiona said, "Or a half-breed like me?"

They were staunch for her. "You look Italian." Their tone was to comfort her.

In exasperation, Fiona put her hands up and waggled them, and her Italian kin smiled at her unknowing confirmation of their reassurance.

She marched off to her mother's room, trailed by Tomas who stood again outside the door.

Maria Evans was in pain. It was not horrendous, but she was hurting. So Fiona hurt.

Her mother asked, "Benjamin?"

And Fiona replied, "His body clock is age three. He sleeps at odd times and is up at night."

"You stay with him?" she inquired with slowly spoken words.

"Yes." Fiona sighed. "For ten more days. They will have to find someone else in that time. I have a job. It's one I like. I want to get back to it."

Her mother frowned. "You do not like Benjamin?"

"I love Benjamin. But I didn't go to school to baby-sit. I want to get back to my job."

"What is wrong with baby-sitting? Child care? Do you think it's degrading?"

Her own mother did that. "No."

"Then why can't you help with Benjamin until I get back? If you don't help, someone else will take my place. How can I go back and take a job away from someone else? After I get back, you can return to your job."

Fiona was shocked. "I can't ask to be allowed leave for all that time. Six months? How can I expect my job to be there after six months?"

"It won't be that long."

"You lie there in bed, in pain, with a reconstructed hip, and you say you'll be back, taking care of Benjamin in less than six months?"

Her own mother looked at her coldly. "Yes."

Fiona tried for clarification. "I am an individual. I am not your replacement. I am filling in for you at this time. It is not easy, but I am doing it. Asking that I do this for six months is unreasonable. You are expecting too much from me. I need my job. I cannot take off six months just to accommodate you."

In Italian, her own mother accused, "You are an Evans. A pinch-mouthed, selfish non-Italian. I should have known I could not count on your loyalty."

"Mother!"

"Never mind." Her very own mother lifted a frail, stopping hand. "I may be able to find another job. At my age . . ." Her voice faltered.

"You don't NEED a job! You only go to the compound so that you may teach Benjamin English and Italian. You—"

Her own mother accused her. "You could teach him."

"*I have a job!*"

Her own mother was dramatic. She turned her face away from her child and said bravely in Italian, "I will lose my job because my child cannot give me six months of her time. Not even does that match the nine months I carried her within my body and suffered the pains of childbirth to give her life. Or all the years I have spent nurturing her, giving her compassion when she was sick and troubled. No. I release you from any obligation you may feel toward your mother."

And Fiona burst into tears.

"Ah, you weep small crocodile tears. You will never know the tears and prayers I have spent on you. Through your illnesses and through the dating time, when you were so young and green. How many times have I lit candles and asked the saints to watch over you? And now all that I ask of you is this tiny favor of six months of this long life I have given you.''

Fiona looked up from her handkerchief. ''You've overdone it,'' she said in English. ''You should have quit when you were ahead.''

Her mother looked back at her child and raised her eyebrows. ''You were sold?''

''Not entirely. But you've blown it. I'll do the ten days. That's all.'' She drew a wavering breath and blew her nose.

Her own mother considered. ''I suppose I can go by ambulance each day.''

''Nine days.'' Fiona subtracted one.

''No. No. Ten days.''

''Father has put up with you all this time?''

With oxygen at her nose and tubes running into her arms, wearing the hospital gown and her hair combed by a stranger, her mother smiled a little. ''There've been fringe benefits.''

''You are outrageous.''

''I love you.'' Her mother demurred. ''I want what's best for you.''

Fiona wasn't really listening, and scoffed. ''So you enlist me to baby-sit another woman's child?''

''You could be a good influence there.''

''He's too young.'' Fiona shook her head. ''He wouldn't remember my influence after only six months.''

''Take care of Benjamin.''

How many times had her mother asked that in these past couple of days? She was probably going through the change and had a menopausal feeling of motherhood toward the boy.

Fiona gave her mother an evaluating look, but just then she saw the involuntary flinch of pain in her mother's eyes. It tore a hole in Fiona's heart. She said, "I'll stay with Benjamin for the ten days, and...we'll see. You'll be home by then, Dad will have to go back to work, and you may need me with you."

"I have Alfred." Her voice was thin, as if she were exhausted.

Alfred was Maria's youngest. Her eldest, Fiona, rose, saying, "He can't give you a bath. And he needs to be at school all day."

Maria put one hand carefully to her forehead, rattling the various monitoring connections along her hand. "Well, as you say, we'll see."

"I love you, Mother."

"I know."

"I'll be back tomorrow," Fiona promised.

"Bring Benjamin with you."

A little jealous, Fiona said, "Yes." She leaned to kiss her mother's cheek. "I do love you."

"I know that."

Fiona kissed her again. "You are a harpy."

Her mother smiled a little, but her eyes were pain-filled.

"You have an unfair advantage. How can I think of myself and my own life, when you are in pain?"

"It's all I have to work with." That was Maria's puzzling reply.

"You are shameless," Fiona accused her own mother.

"I know." Her mother closed her eyes.

Fiona's eyes were filled with tears of sentiment as she left the side of her mother's bed, walked across the room and opened the door to walk right into Tomos.

He did not really notice. He had blocked the door with his body as he crowded the nurse who was looking up at Tomas. Her cheeks were pink and her eyes sparkled.

She made Fiona feel irritated. Fiona went on back to the waiting room, to find that her father had gone to work. He could go to work, while Fiona was expected to baby-sit her mother's charge. Her mother was Italian. If Fiona had been male, her mother would never have dreamed of having her stay with a child who had how many adults around underfoot "guarding" him.

Why couldn't all those people keep an eye on the boy at the same time?

Women's liberation had not yet reached to the Evans household. Fiona was subjected to outdated rules. But she was a woman. She was her own woman.

She did not even notice her guard had been changed from Tomas to Nick. It had been done while she had said goodbye to the relatives in the waiting room, taking their turns cheering up Maria Evans . . . or Maria Garibaldi, as their prejudice dictated.

Nick followed along after Fiona, down to the elevator, through the corridor and out to the parking lot. He waited as she unlocked the car door and he saw her safely inside the car. He smiled and waved her off as he removed his driver's license from his wallet.

Sure enough, as Fiona exited the parking lot, she noted there was a cop waiting at Nick's car.

With a distinct feeling of grimness, Fiona returned to the compound. Checked in, she parked her car in the visitor's space and opened her door. Benjamin was there, squealing her name and laughing. "You're home!"

Home? She stretched her mouth into an insincere smile.

Then her glance was drawn up, and she saw Dominic Lorenzo watching her.

How dared he?

He came over to her, picked up the wiggling Benjamin and said pleasantly, "How is your mother?"

"In pain." Her voice was taut.

"Ah-h-h."

How did he make the sound so sympathetic? How had he known to do only that? He was a manipulator.

In English, he asked, "Are you very tired? Would you like to change and go for a swim? The water is warm. The current has shifted so we have some warm surface water. I told Benjamin that he had to wait for you. Benjamin, ask her nicely."

Benjamin laughed. "She will. It will make me sleepy." He deliberately gave her a darling glance. "Will you swim?"

She could do this. It would just be the two of them. "All right. Come, let's change."

Dominic set the boy down and said, "See? If you ask nicely, she will go."

Fiona was walking toward the porch and behind her back Benjamin looked up at his father as he reached his hand up. Dominic put a finger to his lips and shook his head. Benjamin grinned, turned and ran after Fiona.

So, when Fiona and Benjamin arrived at the beach, it was with some shock that Fiona found Dominic already there, in swim trunks and already in the water.

Well, that did not mean she needed to be around him. He could take care of Benjamin, and she would swim.

She waded into the lake and Benjamin laughed out loud. A child's laughter is infectious. She looked back at him and laughed.

He reached his arms to her and said, "Up."

She could not resist. She took him into her arms and waded deeper into the water, jumping the warm, gentle waves. It was glorious.

She could go no farther, or Benjamin would get mouthfuls of water. So she stood, holding him, allowing him to "float" over the waves.

Then Dominic came and said, "I'll take him. Go swim." Taking the boy, Dominic looked around. "Don't go too far out. If you should need me, I'd have to take him in first. So stay within this area." He gestured, showing her, and then he looked at her and smiled.

He was the artists' inspiration for gods of the seas. He looked in his natural element. His hair was roughened by the water, dripping, curling. His eyebrows were thick and unruly. His eyelashes were spiked, and his brown body was beautiful.

Again, she felt the niggling memory of a mermaid and a seal man. She stared, her lips parted, her face very serious.

His eyes narrowed down and he stilled as he watched her.

Fiona saved herself. She did a short dive and swam away underwater. She came up some distance from him, noting only him, and Benjamin was shrieking "Fiona!" as he tried to scramble out of his father's arms.

"Here! Benjamin! I am here."

He looked around his father's head and stared, his face still alarmed.

She swam back to them and said, "I was just swimming underwater. Watch."

She again slipped below the surface and swam only a short distance. She surfaced, and he was watching anxiously. She called, "See?" and noted that Dominic was already pointing to where she would surface.

"Me, too." Benjamin tried to get out of his father's arms.

"No!" Fiona began swimming toward them.

But Dominic showed Benjamin how to hold his breath and duck his head. Then he showed him how to float, keeping the child between his arms and controlling him. They played that way for a long time. Twice Benjamin got a mouthful of water, and he began to understand there was more to lake swimming than just jumping into water.

Fiona swam, free, with the effortless strokes of a practiced swimmer. After the several days of tension and not being at the hospital with her mother, swimming gave Fiona the release that she so badly needed. Then, too, there had been the responsibility of a child that had distracted her from her mother's plight. Fiona swam, the soothing water healing her distress.

She saw that Dominic had put Benjamin onto his shoulders and put the boy's hands to grip his hair as he then swam, keeping his head and Benjamin above the water. Benjamin squealed and laughed.

And there was the flash of Dominic's teeth as he, too, laughed.

Fiona rolled in the water, effortlessly maneuvering to ease herself. The freedom of water. With humans eighty-nine-percent fluids, no wonder they love water. They need to drink water, to see it, to have it close, to be on it or in it. They need it, the feel of it, the sound of it. Perhaps she was a mermaid. And Dominic? Was he a seal man? Curious to look at him, she swam closer to him.

"Don't let go," Dominic warned Benjamin, yet again.

"Let me take him now. I can do that." Fiona went over and reached for the boy.

"No. He about pulls your hair out. He'll make a good horseman. He is already guiding me."

And Fiona laughed.

So, then, did Benjamin.

They went up onto the beach and dried themselves. Fiona was not quite ready to quit, but Benjamin had had enough. Fiona looked back at the water. "It was just what I needed." She was surprised she had said it aloud, but it was true.

"A little more?" Dominic raised his eyebrows. "A bit longer?"

"He needs to go inside. He'll take a good nap."

"Now?" Dominic asked.

"Well, yes. He was up early. He needs to nap for a while or he'll be up at three tomorrow."

"How long should he sleep?"

"An hour."

Dominic turned to the wooded shoreline and whistled shrilly twice.

Fiona asked, "Why did you do that?"

Dominic replied, "Alex will come and take Benjamin inside to nap. You can stay and swim longer. I will watch for you. No one may swim alone."

"No, no," she protested. "I can't take your time."

"I have taken yours. Let me do this."

"I would like to swim for a while." She looked out over the lake water.

"Go in." It was not quite a command. "I will watch."

Alex came and grinned at them, as Dominic put a contented Benjamin into his arms. Dominic was saying, "Take him to the house, upstairs to the middle room on the left, dry him and roll him into bed."

"I have a little brother. I'll rinse him with the hose."

Dominic said, "Good." Then he turned to tell Fiona to go ahead and swim, but she was already in the water. He watched her strokes. She was very good, a competent swimmer. He could not stay on the shore, so he waded into the water. It was easy to go out to her and swim alongside her. It was almost a dance in the water as, separated, they matched strokes...as a mermaid and seal man?

They went out quite far, then stopped to tread water and smile. It was she who decided she should go back to the beach. She began to swim back, and he longed to tow her. To hold her along him and swim back with her. Their strokes were slower.

When they stood at the shoreline and rested just a minute, she looked back over the water. Then she smiled at Dominic. "That was lovely."

In English, he told her, "Mention the sand, it cost so damned much."

"It's prefect."

And he grinned.

But as they came out of the water, she became stiff with him. She moved differently, more self-consciously, not as free. Her face was serious. She said, "My car has never driven so smoothly. What did they do to it?"

"I'll ask Romano."

"I want the bill for the repairs."

Back to that again. He sighed, and debated throwing her back into the lake. She was easier to handle if she was immersed in water. He said again, "I'll ask Romano." Fiona Evans was a nuisance. Why couldn't she just go along with what he wanted? Other women had done that quite comfortably. Why couldn't this one?

She leaned over and rubbed her hair vigorously. He watched her body, her movements. She was exquisite.

She stood up, straightening, and flipped her hair back. He watched it fall down her back and around her shoulders. She took away his breath.

Then she did an awful thing: she took a large towel and wrapped it around her, just under her arms like a long sarong. She had covered herself.

But his glances didn't leave her. She was still eye-catching. She was fascinating. Irritating, but fascinating.

Six

In those following several days, a truce was called. Actually that meant that everyone else acted as they always had, it was Fiona who did not rock the boat. The next day she and Benjamin had gone in her car to the hospital to see her mother, and Nick followed. He had parked as he always did, before he accompanied them to the waiting room.

As they walked into it, Benjamin exclaimed to Tomas, "You are here!"

Tomas picked up the boy and hugged him.

Benjamin leaned back to look at Tomas, his little hands on each side of the man's face. "I have missed you. I did not know where you had gone."

"I was here, taking care of Maria."

"No one said." Benjamin hugged the man. "Will you come back?"

"Yes."

Tomas did not introduce the boy to any of the people. He escorted Benjamin and Fiona down the hall to Maria's room.

Benjamin was glad enough to see Maria, but he was fascinated by the big building. He had to look out of the windows and exclaim at all he could see from that height.

Maria was weepy in her gladness at seeing the child. Fiona decided the menopausal maternal-yearning theory was probably correct.

When they said goodbye, Benjamin hugged Maria's head and about wrenched it sideways. He pronounced, "We will come Friday." He looked at Fiona. "Tomorrow?"

Fiona agreed. "Tomorrow."

In the hall, Tomas gave the visitors back to Nick, who then returned them to Fiona's car, and they drove home. Benjamin couldn't sit still, there was so much to see. So many cars. And TRUCKS!

Fiona figured no one had ever taken the child anywhere. Well, she would.

She realized that she would have to get permission from Momma. Back at the house Fiona approached Momma, who listened with great interest, bending an intense look on Fiona all during her explanation, then she said, "Ask Lorenzo."

"You run the house," Fiona declared.

Momma retorted, "He is Lorenzo's child. He will not agree to this. I will not go against Lorenzo."

No argument there. So Fiona went along with the happenstance schedule that Benjamin's three-year-old clock dictated. She did not upset the applecart. She waited for the right time to ask Dominic for his child's release from the imprisonment of the compound.

They did swim. The current was comparatively warm in those September days, and Benjamin's frolicking was exuberant. Whenever they went to the beach, Dominic showed up magically.

It was not magic. Romano had been instructed to call Dominic and tell him when Fiona and Benjamin were going to the beach. And Dominic drove home and arrived at the beach in swimming trunks.

Because of Benjamin's weird scheduling, their swim was never at the same time of the day, so Dominic could always be surprised to see them. He would stop walking and say, "Well, here you are!" And he spoke in English.

Benjamin loved it. He laughed and began to run to Dominic, just like kids are supposed to run to their fathers. And Fiona realized that until then the two had been strangers.

Fiona figured it probably had been Maria's fall that had called Dominic's attention to Benjamin. That was probably right. And she looked at the man, to find him watching her with an enigmatic expression, as if he was considering which part of her to bite? He looked hungry. She said, "You haven't eaten."

"No." He smiled at her.

"Then you can swim." She gave permission.

He loved it. "Thank you."

"I am teaching Benjamin that one does not go into the water right after eating."

He had the gall to say, "That's been disproven."

She lifted her nose. "It's a longtime rule, the other is only theory."

"I see."

She glanced up. His eyes smoldered. How could they possibly?

Get 4 Books FREE

SEE BACK OF CARD FOR DETAILS

DETACH ALONG DOTTED LINE AND MAIL TODAY! – DETACH ALONG DOTTED LINE AND MAIL TODAY! – DETACH ALONG DOTTED LINE AND MAIL TODAY!

BUSINESS REPLY CARD

FIRST CLASS MAIL   PERMIT NO. 717   BUFFALO, NY

POSTAGE WILL BE PAID BY ADDRESSEE

SILHOUETTE READER SERVICE
3010 WALDEN AVE
P O BOX 1867
BUFFALO NY 14240-9952

NO POSTAGE
NECESSARY
IF MAILED
IN THE
UNITED STATES

He wanted to lay her down in the sand and have his way with her. What could they do with Benjamin? Kids should come in containers, so that they could be put away when they were not convenient. Neutrally, he inquired, "What are you building?"

She gave him a surprised glance. "A sand castle."

"Ah-h-h. You need water."

"Benjamin is 'water boy.' He keeps us supplied." She gave Dominic a telling look. "It's good exercise."

He laughed without opening his mouth. "He was awake last night?"

She bowed her head in agreement. "For two hours."

"Why didn't you call me?" he asked rashly. "I could have helped."

"You weren't yet home."

"Oh." He licked his lips. "Yes."

"Are you courting her?"

"Courting?" He tasted the word as if he did not know its meaning.

"Do you marry this one?"

"No." There was a long silence. Benjamin came busily back with a half bucket of water that was mostly liquid sand. He dumped that on the growing castle and went back for more. Dominic figured now was a good time to explain himself to her, so he said, "I have had two wives. I'm not a man who takes to marriage. My business takes my time."

"Not Benjamin?"

Dominic looked over to the boy who was busily dipping the bucket into the lapping waves. "He is a good boy."

She recognized that as a nothing reply. She thinned her lips in censure, but she did refrain from scolding him. That was a part of the truce rules she had set for herself. She was not in that household to reorder it and straighten out the relationships. But she did mean to get Benjamin off the compound, so that he could see some of the world. She must remember she was there for only seven more days.

She said, "I have to go the library. May I take Benjamin with me?"

"And Nick."

She took a slow breath. "Yes."

"You may."

"Thank you." Her gratitude did not sound sincere, even to her own ears.

Gently he said, "I will stay with the boy. Go swim. I'll whistle when it's my turn. Like this." He gave one short whistle and one long. That was the signal on the compound for Fiona. If there were two short ones after that, it would mean she was in danger.

She smiled a little, even before she looked up. "You don't mind?"

"No."

"Just for ten minutes. It would be a treat."

He cautioned her. "Stay within the bounds I set. If you needed me, I would have to whistle for Alex. You understand."

"I'll be all right. But I will stay within the bounds. Thank you."

She gave him a smile that almost paralyzed him, but he did manage to sound fairly natural as he promised, "I'll whistle for you in twenty minutes."

She ran down to the water, and his soul soared with watching the beauty of that. But then he had to scramble to keep Benjamin from following her into the water. He said, "No."

Benjamin dodged and ran into the water, and Dominic allowed it. Keeping close, he allowed Benjamin to discover that he could not yet swim in such water.

Dominic scooped up the boy and turned him upside down as he patted his back while the boy coughed and lake water ran from his nose.

Dominic stood Benjamin down on the sand and squatted beside the boy as he cried. Benjamin quieted, and even then Dominic used the English. "We live near this water." He gestured to the lake. "You must learn how it is to go into the water without knowing how to swim. We have all told you that. Yet you tried it again. Now you know. You will learn to swim. Then you will practice. You will be able to swim like a fish, but it takes time. Do you understand?"

Benjamin nodded.

"Come. I will help you begin."

Benjamin's hold on his father's neck was choking. Gradually, Dominic distracted the boy until he was playing within the limits of freedom Dominic allowed.

Even then, Dominic had kept the flashing arms of Fiona in sight. He monitored her the entire time. And when a half hour had passed, he whistled.

She waved. As she swam in toward the shore, Dominic stood up, holding Benjamin. "Watch her. See how she moves her arms? She learned to do that. She practiced. You, too, will learn."

And Benjamin watched differently.

She rose from the water like a dark-haired Venus on her half shell. Her hair was tossed and dripping, and her suit clung to her lovely body. She looked back at the water and said, "It is so wonderful." Then she picked up her towel and dried her face. "Ah-h-h." She closed her eyes and sighed in contentment.

He wanted it to be his body that would draw just such a satisfied sound from her. She was committed to seven more days—exactly long enough to sate himself in her. Then she would leave of her own accord, and he would be free again. Free of this bemusement that was so strange.

"Go swim," she said. "I shall watch for you."

And showing off, Dominic ran down the sand to launch himself in a flat dive that was exquisite. Fiona's lips parted in a gasp of pleasure, and she watched as his powerful arms propelled him through the water.

"He's better." Benjamin gave her a judging look as he used English words.

She followed his use of English. "So will you be better one day."

"It looks . . . easy." He had found the word.

"It is easy, once you know how to do it. It's like using a spoon. Once you just used your fingers."

"And I was MESSY!" He admitted that with some satisfaction.

"Were you?"

"Yes!" And Benjamin laughed.

They worked on the castle, with Benjamin toting the water and Fiona watching Dominic. "Do you see him?" she would ask Benjamin in English.

"He's okay."

"But where is he?"

And Benjamin would stop and look for his father. "There." He would point.

"Yes."

When Dominic came back up to the beach, he had swum only about fifteen minutes. Swimming was not as interesting as watching Fiona.

She sassed, "Tired already?"

He knew she needed to be chased around and caught. His wet lashes closed down on the intenseness of his eyes and, in English, he said, "I didn't have anyone to set the pace."

She laughed. Even she knew his words were not that funny. His reply was worth maybe a quirk on the lips, at most a slight smile. She just felt like laughing. She realized she was flirting just a little. With him? How shocking. She would have to watch herself.

Dominic carried Benjamin back to the house. He was groggy by the time they got there.

Alex met them, and stuck to Italian. "If you do not rinse him off, Momma will raise hell. Let me." He took the boy into his own arms, and asked, "You did not intend to take all that sand to bed with you, did you?"

Benjamin shook his head, but he smiled.

Alex put the boy down, turned on the hose and began washing Benjamin carefully, taking off his bathing suit and doing a thorough job of it. The cherub turned and helped, watching.

Fiona observed tenderly. Dominic saw that was so.

Alex said easily, "I know how to put him into bed. We will go ahead." He put out a hand to the little boy and said, "All right? Can you make it on your own two feet?"

Benjamin said, "Yes."

Dominic said, near Fiona's ear, "Your turn. Take off your suit and I will rinse you."

The most amazingly shocking thrill that she had ever experienced slid through her body. She gasped with the exciting feel of it. She saw that his eyes were hidden by his lashes and his face was serious. That confused her. He was not teasing her to taunt. He was offering... She snubbed him saucily in English. "Does your mother know you speak to ladies in that way? Shame on you."

He replied in her tongue. "I never had a mother that I knew. I was raised by a series of families. They were all Italian. Would a mother be shocked by a son who wanted a woman?"

He wanted her. He had said it out loud. No one was that bold. Did she walk off in a snit? No. She stood there trying to think of a way to reply that would not sound asinine and prudish. And she knew then that she wanted him.

She faced him and considered that surprising fact. She wanted a taste of him. He was an impossible man. But he lured her. If she could just experience him once, she could know what he would be like, and that would satisfy her. Or would it?

There was the rub. What if a taste of him was not enough? What if she would want more? More of a man who was about as basically male as any man could be? He would not be hanging around, waiting for her to decide if she wanted him. He would be gone.

He had already told her he was not interested in marrying any woman. He had a son. That part of his life was completed. So he wanted only an affair. Should she?

She was old enough to know the ramifications of such a move. She supported herself. She could take care of herself. She was free and self-sustaining. And her body wanted his. That was a dumb reason to do something that intimate.

She would reject his opening.

She tilted her head, looked him over deliberately and, still in English, she said, "You must have to fight women off. You could make a woman go berserk." She smiled then, in an immune manner, and she went to the hose to use the stream to wash the sand off her legs.

He moved near to her, and said, "You were sitting in the sand. We can't have you clogging the plumbing."

She was bent over. She raised her head and gave him an amused look. "Yes, sir."

She turned her back to him, put the hose down her suit and pulled the suit out at the bottom, allowing the water to run over her nakedness, quite freely, and out from under her suit. She did that with practiced efficiency... and some smugness.

He had his hands on his hips, and he said a quiet "Damn."

She laughed. It was a soft woman's laugh. She had not known how to do that, not before then.

That was when he became really determined to have her. The thought of her had enticed him, but it had been only a thought. Now it was determination. He would have her. He would have her sassy and laughing and purring in his bed.

"Benjamin should sleep for a hour," Dominic said to her. "Come with me."

She put him off. "I was up with him last night. I have to nap."

His voice was low and unbending. "Come with me."

"Where?" She turned to look at him.

He was lax and easy. Unthreatening. "I'll show you the winter house."

Yes. And what else would he show her? "I'm dead on my feet. I need to sleep."

And he had the nerve to say in that seducing voice of his, "It's quiet at the winter house. You can nap there."

Airily she inquired, "How would I get back here to waken Benjamin in an hour?"

"I'd wait for you."

She gestured to the house. "I have a bed here. I'll stay here. When Benjamin wakens, we can go then. It would be an adventure for him. Will he remember having lived there last spring?"

Dominic shrugged. "Children's memories are brief. They don't recall much from earlier years."

"When did you come to this house in the spring?"

"In April," he told her. "We move to the winter house the end of October."

She wanted to know, "Did he mind?"

"No."

She studied him for a minute, the water still running over her body. "You are so sure. Are you around him enough to know?"

"They tell me."

She cautioned Dominic. "You are making him care about you. Do you realize that?"

Rather carelessly, he replied, "I've always cared about him. He is my son."

"But he would miss you if you weren't around."

Dominic said, "I would miss him, if he wasn't here."

"But you would know where he was, and he doesn't understand where you are. He was surprised to see Tomas at the hospital. Benjamin hadn't known what had become of Tomas. Has he ever been to your office?"

"No." His reply was short, and he was becoming restless. He frowned a little.

"He was amazed by the *trucks* along the freeway to the hospital. He was exuberant. Why haven't you taken him off the compound?"

"He is only a little boy."

"Waiting for his twenty-first birthday?" Her tone was only half-teasing. She handed him the hose.

He made short shrift of rinsing himself off. "Will you come with me?"

"Thank you, no."

"I see." He turned away and went off toward the back of the house.

She watched after him, feeling his desertion. He had gone off like an irritated man who has been rebuffed. Why hadn't he said, "Perhaps another time?" No. He was used to being courted, to having his way. He was spoiled rotten.

He was a man to avoid. One to treat like a rattlesnake. He was dangerous.

But, ahh, how she would have liked to have . . . Impossible.

When he came home that night, the light was on in her room. They were up. His step lightened as he entered the front door. So he was surprised when he saw that the light was also on in the kitchen.

He went down the hallway silently, to see who was there. Benjamin was dunking cookies in milk. He was a mess. Dominic said to Fiona, "Not a long-enough swim?"

He was in formal clothes and looked gorgeous. She replied to his query, "A cookie attack."

Benjamin said, "Um-umph."

Dominic noted his child. "Hello to you."

Benjamin was not very alert. Alex came through and paused. Dominic said, "Alex." Then he asked, "Would you take Benjamin up to his room? He might—"

But Fiona already had a warm cloth and wiped Benjamin clean. He smiled like the cherub he was, kindly, a benediction. And he went away with Alex.

Dominic's body got excited. It was his first time alone with Fiona. He did not know what to say besides: Come to bed.

She asked, "How was your meeting."

"It wasn't a 'meeting' as such. It was a family gathering. The male part."

"It went your way?" she inquired.

"Naturally."

She tilted her head. "Should it?"

"Yes."

So she asked, "Why?"

"Because... It was logical."

"Logical." She tested the word. "But was it good for them?"

"Them?"

She gestured. "The other side."

"It went as I wanted." And as he wanted, he went to her, pulled her up from the chair into his arms, and kissed her.

It was shattering to be kissed that way. It stunned them both. They made hungry sounds and moved their hands and their bodies. Their attention was riveted, then distracted by the sensations inside them. Their breaths became erratic and their mouths greedy. It was the kind of kiss that writers told about but that ordinary people seldom experienced.

When she was limp and malleable, he set her from him. He was a shambles. His breathing was harsh and his hands trembled. His eyes were flickering fires of desire.

But he deliberately turned and walked away from her.

She put her hand to her forehead and thought she might faint. Good heavens. What an incredible experience! And she had thought that she could toy with something that powerful? What a fool she was!

A very sobered Fiona crept up the stairs, silently so as not to call attention to herself, and quietly went to her room, closed the door and slid into her bed. She lay wide-eyed and stunned. What had she touched? What power had she taunted? She had been a fool.

The cautionings of the moralists were correct. Don't play with fire. She wouldn't... she wouldn't.

Eventually, she slept. And she dreamed the mermaid sought the seal man, and found him. She laughed and splashed him, and he came off that rock—

Fiona wakened to stare soberly out the window at the night.

She heard him as he came quietly up onto the porch. It could have been one of the other prowling men, but she knew his step. When had she learned it? Why had she listened for his step in order to learn it?

She heard him mount the stairs and come to the hall door of Benjamin's room.

Would he come to the open connecting door? If he did, what would she do?

But he turned away and went back to his own room. It was a long time before she slept.

Dominic Lorenzo had done a forbidden thing. Forbidden specifically by himself. He'd gone to the lake and swum. Fiona against his body had been like a hundred thousand bolts of lightning. He'd never experienced anything like her before.

That he wanted her, he'd known soon enough, but to kiss her with such a violent response in him had shaken him. Appalled him. This wasn't a sampling of a woman. This was Fiona. This was serious. How could that be?

Had he wanted her before, now it was a need. A desire so acute that he was almost sick with the hunger. He was stunned.

Exhausted from the swim, he doubled it by taking a hot shower. He went to bed, confident that he'd sleep, and his body's need flooded his mind. He shivered with it. Could he go to her and say, "I have a serious problem. Be a good citizen and help me with it."

She wasn't interested. She'd— But she'd kissed him. Now that he could think past his own reaction to that kiss, she hadn't fought him away. She'd strained against him and murmured in shaky breaths. Her soft body had been tight against his hard body, pressing, squirming. She'd *liked* his kissing. She wanted him!

So.

Now, how was he going to get her? He had to get her away from Benjamin. He had to get her alone. He had to have her.

And he went to sleep plotting, so his dreams were really wild. But it was never Fiona whom he found in his arms. He had not wanted anyone else. He searched for her. Only for Fiona.

He wakened rather haggard. How long had it been since he had wakened tired? He did not need sleep. He needed it today. He called in to his office and said he would be in later. When had he ever done that?

He jolted the whole house staff by showing up for breakfast. He sat down, and everyone was silent. He made conversation, using his skill with people, and soon he had them all talking and laughing.

It was to that scene that Fiona and Benjamin came. As he had intended, she came upon a jolly "family" breakfast table of diverse men . . . and Dominic Lorenzo.

Benjamin was lifted into his chair next to Romano. The only vacant place for Fiona was next to Dominic. He rose, and so did all the men, and he held her chair.

Amid the greetings, Momma began to dish up more food for her assistants to serve those at the table.

Under all the sounds and talk, Dominic watched Fiona blush as she thanked him for his help with her chair, and he was grimly satisfied that she had blue circles under her eyes. She hadn't had enough sleep, either. Served her right. Any woman who kissed a man like that and didn't give him peace, should look that way.

He slid another glance at her and saw that she suffered. She was embarrassed and uncomfortable. He wanted to hold her hand and soothe her. His reaction to her wasn't her fault. She'd shunned him and annoyed him and bossed him ever since she'd come there. She had never once flirted with him. Well, there had been that laugh and the way she'd put that hose down her suit.

She ate very primly. As the men began to excuse themselves and leave the table, she peeked quickly at Dominic and she did have his attention, so she asked, "After we see my mother, may I take Benjamin to the library today?"

Again he added, "With Nick."

"All right." She had again agreed.

He smiled at her and melted her into a puddle of want. How could he do that to her? She needed to get away from there. After today, there would be six more days for her to get through. She was appalled. In just six days, she would have to leave? Oh, no. Oh, how could she? And she looked at him with large, stricken eyes.

She rocked him back on his heels . . . and he was sitting on a chair. Think of the impact that caused him to feel he was teetering on his heels while sitting there! He could not breathe. He willed his lungs to try. They had forgotten how to coordinate. He looked aside, and without Fiona to distract him he could breathe.

Why had she looked at him that way? It was as if she were going to cry. What was the matter? He put his hand on her shoulder and asked quietly in her English, "Are you all right?"

"I'm not sure."

"What's wrong?" he asked in soft alarm.

She repeated, "I'm not sure."

And a smile sneaked out and curled his lips just a little. He was not the only one suffering. It was only a matter of time until their shared problem would be solved.

Seven

After a time, Dominic noticed that everyone had left the kitchen, and Benjamin had gone on some errand of his own. Dominic and Fiona sat alone in silence. She was still twiddling with her breakfast, looking sad and unsettled. She sighed. He reached for her opposite shoulder, turned up her face with the other hand, and he kissed her.

That sort of kiss was probably what had started the universe. The big bang? An explosion of passion shook their very souls. It must have rattled the windows and knocked the house from its foundation.

Her weak neck allowed her to lay her head on his shoulder and she became inert. On the other hand, he was a tangle of nerves. He shivered, his hands shook and his breathing was erratic. Even his lips trembled.

If she'd had just a little more control, she would have been alarmed for him. She moved her lips to attempt speech, and he kissed her again.

She wanted to drag him under the table and assault him. But she was restrained from such rash behavior by her mother's training. "You must not!" How many times had Fiona heard that. It was ingrained in her very skull. She moaned in protest.

He thought she was objecting to his kisses and pulled his head back to look at her.

She was boneless and pale.

"Fiona? Are you all right?"

And *she* whispered, "Not yet."

He about went off like a skyrocket!

He didn't know what to do next. He didn't! He gasped and struggled to just function in order to keep his life support system going. He said, "Awrk."

She nodded in a disorganized way.

Then he said very seriously, "Fiona—" But he didn't know what else to say. He could only think of taking her to his room and barricading the door for a week.

Momma banged a pan, emptying it in the trash. She called to someone in her usual no-nonsense manner, then she stomped up the few steps to the back porch. She rattled the back doorknob before she opened it and came inside. There she stopped and looked at the separated, silent pair at the table.

Fiona's eyes were either closed or she was staring at her plate. She was very pale, but her lips were puffed and quite red.

Dominic shifted restlessly in his chair and took quick glances at Fiona. He shuffled his feet and smoothed his hair.

With satisfaction, Momma slammed pots around, then brought the coffeepot over. "More?"

Both shook their heads.

Fiona started to rise, and Dominic quickly helped her with her chair as he also stood up. They left the room without speaking.

The pair did not notice how quiet the kitchen became. They did not hear the floor squeak as Dominic stopped Fiona, listening, looking around before his gaze came back to her.

His stare was so intense that it burned into her eyes and flamed down inside her body to her core. How could that be? It was true. She licked her lips, but couldn't control her tongue, and it was not an efficient accomplishment, but he watched, fascinated.

And he kissed her again.

The floor creaked as their feet shuffled while they tried to get closer and still keep their balance. His breathing was like the beginning pump-up of a steam calliope. And in the kitchen, Momma began to bang pans and sing.

The two at the bottom of the stairs ended the kiss reluctantly, their hearts running away inside their chests, their bodies tingling, hurting hungry. One touch would set them off.

They stared at each other in sensual shock, stunned by the scope of their desire, sobered by it.

He held her shoulders until he was sure she could stand by herself. Then he took a dragging step back from her to stare at her. He could not think. He was drowned in just feeling, awareness, wanting... caution. What was happening to him?

She gestured with a floppy hand and moved her lips, but no sound came. She felt he had understood, and she went carefully up the stairs, her head down, her steps slow. She was a zombie.

He watched until she was out of sight. Then he looked around, trying to figure out where he was and what he was supposed to be doing. He did not know, so he went to his office.

Fiona asked her guardian angel for help. She wandered around her room for a while, shading the request. After all, she had six days, and what could happen in just six days? She wanted more of those kisses. She erased the plea. She breathed in and out with deliberation. Her brain gradually cleared, and she looked around.

Then she called to Benjamin and they did their morning chores, making their beds and changing clothing so that they could go see her mother. It was then that Fiona remembered today was cleaning day and everything had to be up off the floor. They did that.

But eventually, Fiona and Benjamin went off on his great adventure. On the freeway leading to the hospital, he exclaimed over the trucks. He had had no idea they were so big. He had trucks of all sizes, but they were his size. These were BIG! He loved them.

They went to see Fiona's mother who was taking exercises very bravely. Then they went to the library, followed by Nick. He had said, ''Why won't you let me drive you? Why use two cars? I could lose you in this traffic.''

She had smiled.

He said, ''Don't you dare.'' When she went on smiling, he warned, ''Don't even think about it. If I should lose you, Lorenzo would kill me. He'd take me out in the woods, and I'd have to dig my own grave.

Dying wouldn't be so bad, but digging your own grave gives you time to think on your sins. Don't do that to me."

Fiona had sighed in resignation and told him exactly how to get to the Chicago Public Library Cultural Center just off Michigan on West Washington. And she told him about the parking spaces available. Nick had never been there.

They went inside the building, and Nick and Benjamin were impressed. They looked around, and Fiona had to slow her steps so that they could keep up.

Then she noticed a very big, rough man come in after them. He looked at her so piercingly, that she was sure he knew her scars and moles. She was glad that Nick was there.

How silly. She was in a public place. Nothing could happen to her there. She was perfectly safe. She gave another indifferently calm look at the man.

He was no longer watching her, so she could examine him. He was formidable. Big. She bet he had been in more than his share of street fights. He looked that way. As if he knew how to fight dirty if he had to do it. He could take care of himself.

Fiona shivered a little and went on about her business.

However, she was not too surprised when she was back in the stacks and that same big man approached her. He said something to her, and she did not at first understand him.

Then she realized that he was being courteous and had said, "Excuse me."

She stepped back for him to go past, then she understood that he had meant "pardon me," and he wanted to speak to her. She waited cautiously. Where was Nick?

And Nick was there. He said to the larger man, "Whatcha want?" in an only-through-me voice.

Scrambling his words so that his listeners had to sort through for clues, the man basically said, "Name's Finnig. I'm a friend of Kevin McBride. He's worried about her. You Fiona Evans, right?"

Nick said, "It's none of your business."

Fiona said, "Ni-ick. Kevin's my boss. Tell him I'm just fine. I'll be in touch today."

Finnig used his chin to indicate Nick, as he said to Fiona, "He got a gun on you?"

She bubbled laughter. "No." And she laughed again. "You tell Kevin that his worry is from his imaginative Irish blood. I'm just fine. I'm helping my mother in a—"

Nick ordered, "Don't tell him nothing."

She shrugged. "This isn't as it looks." She lifted her hands out, palms up. "I'm perfectly free." But even as she said it, she wondered if that was really true. But there was being a captive and there was being captivated. There was a difference.

More gently, Fiona reassured Finnig. "Tell Kevin I'm here of my own choice. I will call him today."

Finnig held out a card. "Here's a number. Call it, if you need somebody. Understand? Memorize it now, while I'm here, to see he lets you do it."

Fiona studied the number, then replied, "Thank you. I appreciate the fact that Kevin worried about me enough to be sure."

Finnig looked Nick over dismissively, nodded to Fiona, and walked away.

Nick said, "We gotta talk."

She said, "Your grammar is better in Italian."

"Listen to me. Don't mention Lorenzo to anyone. This is serious. Don't say where you're staying, or who hired you, or who your mother works for, or who Benjamin really is. Understand? Fiona, this is important. We didn't know you'd get loose or we'd've told you sooner. Loose lips sink ships."

She was amazed. "Why do you keep such tight security? It is unusual."

"We've got lots of money. That's like honey for crooked bees. We got to protect Lorenzo and now, Benjamin. You know what kidnappers do to get money? They send back parts of the kid. Pay attention. Don't say anything about the compound, or where it is, or who you live with. Understand, Fiona? You have to understand this is very serious."

"Okay. I really didn't know."

"We keep it that way. But there are people who know the name. Don't spread it around. Be careful. Don't talk about him."

"He's the prisoner." She was struck by that. "He isn't free."

He shrugged, accepting the reality of her words.

"How terrible."

"There's good and bad." Nick put out a hand to indicate the world.

"And there's danger to him."

Nick watched her, weighing her. "Yeah. You could make a bundle giving out just the information you have. Who he is and where he lives. Just the newspapers, for starters." And she was shocked by that, offended. It was there in her startled, angry eyes. Nick was satisfied. He said, "You done here?"

"Almost." Then she said sadly, "No wonder Benjamin hasn't been off the compound. No wonder he's never seen any trucks."

Nick shrugged. "Everybody's life is different."

"He ought to give the money away," she said stubbornly.

Nick laughed. "He's a corporation. Do you know how many people he supports? He has to work his tail off to keep us all going."

"There must be an easier way to live."

"Lorenzo likes it this way." But Nick was pleased with her. She wasn't after Dominic's money. Nick left her and retrieved Benjamin from where he had been stashed under a table that was in sight.

That was what finally made Fiona understand. Benjamin had been taught to stay "stashed" where he had been put. He did not move until Nick gave him the all clear. That was very sobering to witness.

It was almost noon when they returned to the compound. Fiona put their books to one side and went into the library to phone Kevin before he left for lunch.

"Fiona!" he exclaimed. "Are you okay?"

"I met . . . was his name Finnig?"

"Yes. Are you all right?"

"Of course. Why did you worry?"

"I hadn't heard from you, and the contact at the hospital didn't know where you were. Your father gave me no information, at all, and I decided you were being held for ransom. I wanted to help."

"How very kind you are."

"Fiona . . . I've missed you. Can I see you?"

"Well, perhaps I can get down to the office in a few days. I'm quite involved with . . ." She looked up and was pierced by Dominic's watching. He was just coming into the room.

Kevin said, "Fiona?"

"Yes, Kevin."

"What were you saying?"

"I don't remember, but thank you for worrying about me. I feel safer now. I'll see you in a couple of days."

They said goodbye and hung up. She put the phone back in its cradle and looked again at Dominic.

"You feel unsafe?" He almost snarled the Italian words.

This was no time to bait him. She, too, spoke in Italian. "No."

"You told—Kevin—that you now feel safe. So you felt unsafe."

She smiled. He was acting jealous! She explained. "A man came to me at the library—"

"Nick said so. A 'Finnig.' Do you know him?"

"Not until today. He—"

"He gave you a phone number to memorize. What was it?"

"Dominic..." Her lips had said his name out loud. She licked them and smiled.

His name said by her had gone into his body with the intense awareness that she had said it. But his black look was still on her, commanding she answer. "Do I frighten you?"

"Of course not, silly."

He stiffened.

She went to him and laid her hand on his arm, looking up at him. "I was thanking my boss for worrying about me enough to send someone to check on my safety. The man was something. Big. He scared me a—"

"Where was Nick?" he asked harshly, appalled she had been approached by a stranger and that he had not been there with her.

"Right there." She soothed. "Like a genie from a lamp. Poof! He was there. And he stood up to Finnig. You would have been proud of him."

"And Benjamin?"

"'Stashed.'"

"Nick said he told you to be silent about us, this place, Benjamin. I ask it of you."

"I shall comply. I would not harm any of you."

"We only caution you."

"I do understand that. And, Dominic, Kevin is a good boss. He is as concerned for his employees as you are for yours."

"You have no feeling for him?"

"Yes. Loyalty."

With her first word, Dominic's head had come up sharply, then he almost smiled with the second word. "You may be loyal to him."

"Thank you," she said with some irony.

"You are welcome. Come. It is time for lunch."

She started past him. He took her left arm with his left hand high up near her armpit and he stopped her. "I should have been with you."

"I was all right."

"I would protect you." He was very earnest. He pulled her close to him and the back of his hand pressed into her soft breast. "I want you." As tense and wound-up as he was, he kissed her lips very softly. It was a thrilling contrast.

Her eyes were enormous. She was a little scared. She
had had no idea he would come right out and say that
to her so seriously. She had thought he might coax and
tease, but he had said it again and deliberately. What
did women say now? Probably with him they'd all said
yes. Had any of them said no to him? Could she?

Her blue-green eyes, with wide, wide pupils, moved
as she looked over his marvelous face. She studied his
eyes, his mouth, and she wanted him to kiss her again.

He said, "Come." And he led her into the kitchen,
where the men rose from their places as Fiona was
seated next to Dominic. She had the vague impres-
sion that she noted Benjamin again sat next to Romano.

What they had to eat was lost on Fiona. She was
served, she put food into her mouth and chewed.
There was talk around the table, she heard the sounds
but she did not register what anyone was saying. She
heard the rumble of Dominic's voice, on occasion. She
knew that he monitored her. She felt the electric touch
of each glance he gave her.

She was so self-conscious that she was very precise.

Again, everyone had left the table but Fiona and
Dominic. He put one arm along the back of her chair
and the other on the table, almost enclosing her without touching her. "Come with me to see the winter
house."

"I do not dare."

"Why not?"

She shook her head.

He accused her. "You do not trust me."

She whispered softly, "I do not trust myself."

He groaned deep inside himself and leaned his head
over onto his arm that was on the back of her chair.

His head, then, was alongside hers, and she put her cheek against his and slowly rubbed his, with tenderness.

"Fiona." His voice was anguished.

"You must leave me alone. I cannot endure this temptation."

"Do you realize what you are doing to me?"

That provoked her. "And what about me? Do you think I am enjoying this torment?"

Very softly, his deep voice asked, "Is it torment for you?"

"I am not ice."

"Let me know your fire," he coaxed in an unsteady voice.

"Stop this." Her words wavered.

"If you are torturing me, hoping that I will marry you, I will not. Two wives were enough."

Slowly, she got up and left him there. However, without permission, she took a quick peek as she exited the room. His head was still on his arm, and he looked so vulnerable. It was all she could do not to go back to him. But she straightened her spine and went in search of Benjamin.

Scheduled naps were an exercise in futility. Benjamin sneaked out of bed and played quietly in his room. Fiona lay sad-eyed and suffering. It began to rain. How appropriate.

Alex came upstairs and knocked on Fiona's door. She was clothed, and went to open it. "Could Benjamin go out to the barn? We've found the kittens. Lorenzo said it was all right. We'll bring Benjamin back in time for supper."

She nodded. It would do the boy good to be away from her. Alex suggested a sweater and a cap. She

found those things, and watched them down the hall.
Benjamin was questioning about cats. He did not
know about cats?

She straightened Benjamin's room, picking up the
toys and pulling the bed covers taut. After that, she
returned to her own room, went over and looked out
over the rain-dripping trees. For her mood, it was the
perfect day. She was a little cool and got a sweater.
That was when she saw Dominic. He was in sweats and
was running free and easy.

She languished for some time. The gloomy day
matched her pensive mood. She thought of her being
there, and agreed with herself that she was really in a
muddle. She had six more days to go. How was she to
survive?

Moony, she looked out the window, feeling melancholy... and she saw Dominic return. He was walking as if it were not pouring rain. He did not appear to
notice that he was sopping wet. She heard him come
up on the porch steps, in the door, up the stairs of that
empty, silent house and down the hall to his room.

While she could still function as an adult woman,
she would go to him and tell him that she could not
stay. Determined, she rose, walked through the open
door into Benjamin's room, out his open hall door
and down to Dominic's open door. She stopped in the
doorway.

He was naked. He was looking down, his chin on
his chest, his mouth open as he dried his hairy chest.

Mesmerized by his beauty, she watched silently.

Slowly, slowly, his head turned and he looked at her,
his hand slowing. His eyes were pitch-dark and shad-
owed more by his wet lashes. His face was almost
gaunt.

Her lips parted as she watched his body react to her. Then she raised her stare to look into his eyes. It was as if time were suspended. They were the only two people in the world. There was nothing outside of that room.

Moving with the slow motion of a dream, he came to her, took her arm and drew her gently into his room. Then with his stare still on her face, he closed his bedroom door. Inside Fiona's skull, the slight sound of the door closing was like that of the falling rock slabs that sealed the pharaoh's tomb.

He kissed her, and it was so stunning that he inhaled roughly as he continued the kiss, holding her crushed against him. He began to tremble and his body became like steel. His arms and chest, his thighs, his sex. And against his earnest, purposeful maneuvering, she was disorganized mush.

He took her to his bed, but there was the slightest sound, so he moved her to the thick rug. And all the while he was removing her clothing, not a word was said.

She did not recall helping him, at all, but she was naked by the time her back was on the rug. She was marginally amazed by that. But he kissed her mouth, her throat, her breasts, and his hands petted her and caressed and worshiped her.

He deliberately drove her mad.

She loved the feel of his hairy body against hers, his hairy legs moving over her smooth ones. That was just right. She loved to feel his hands on her, and she squirmed and stretched so that he reached all of her. And her own hands ventured, not boldly, but down his naked back feeling the corded muscles. Her hands felt over his hairy chest, then along his cheeks and the rims of his ears, she caressed him, and she slid her fingers into his hair.

He was too needy to delay. He was a shambles. His hands shook and his body shivered. His breaths rasped in his throat. But he could not get enough of having her there for him. He relished her.

When he parted from her to find a condom, she made little gasps of protest, and he returned to her to kiss her again. Still wet from the rain, he was sweating. It was sweat because it was so hot. He had some trouble rolling on the condom because his hands trembled so badly. He had to discard the first one and get another.

Then he came to her. He kissed her again. He still said nothing. He just went ahead. But she was silent. She gave no protest. She helped. She wiggled around to get him more comfortable and she pressed up to help him. So it was, as her barrier was broken, that he realized she had been a virgin. That only inflamed him.

He pressed into her and she grunted and gasped, but he buried himself completely. She was astonished. Then she began to relax as he fought for control. She said, "Well..." rather brightly. She said, "How amazing."

He kissed her. He kissed her deeply, coaxing her, encouraging her. She began to claw at his back and rub the insides of her thighs along the sides of his hips, and she wiggled.

She arched her back to press her breasts harder against him. She hugged him tightly to her, and was very aware of how they were coupled. She moved a little and the mating was more comfortable, more exciting.

He groaned and chuffed. He said, "Hold still." He warned, "Do not move." He moaned, "Fiona." He kissed along her ear and slipped his tongue inside the shell of it, giving her goose bumps all over and setting off shivers deep inside her.

He said, "I cannot last any longer."

She said, "Oh?"

He said, "Fiona."

She kissed along his ear and poked her sassy tongue inside it, just as he had done to hers.

He said, "Be careful."

"Do you like that? I liked it when you did that to me."

"I am about to explode."

"Now? Not yet. I want to feel this." She stretched her legs straight, unfortunately squeezing at just the wrong time, and he did indeed explode. But she rode with his wildness and her passion burst just after his. They clutched each other tightly, as they crossed that magic line and held together through the free-fall into paradise.

As they lay in a tangle on his rug, they slowly came back to reality. And she wept just a little.

"Did I hurt you?"

"No." She shook her head a tiny bit.

"Why do you weep?"

She fumbled to explain. "It was just so...amazing. So...emotional."

He patted her and soothed her, murmuring sweet words in Italian.

Who would dream such an aloof man could be so tender?

"It was wonderful. Thank you." He kissed her cheek. "You are so sweet. I cannot believe you are here. I had no hope."

"I wanted you, too." She was honest.

He eased from her and leaned to kiss her yet again as he said, "Lie still." He went into the bathroom, and when he returned he carried a warm cloth. He washed her very gently. He kissed her very sweetly. "Are you all right?"

She stretched and smiled at him. "Much better."

He watched her. "You amaze me. You are so honest with me. You don't pout and pretend. You let me know that you wanted me, too. I almost went wild wanting you. I could not sleep or think straight." He put the cloth aside and lay down beside her. "You are so beautiful. Do you know what it did to me to have you put that damned hose down your suit?"

"I did it from the top," she protested. "There was nothing lascivious about that."

"You have driven me crazy."

"You helped me not at all. You have learned to kiss very well. Have you had a whole flock of women?"

"Are you comparing women to hens?"

"No. I just want to know if you have been very... active."

"No. I am not even skilled at putting on a condom."

"That surprises me. Did you not use protection ordinarily?"

"I have slept with very few women, but they generally took care of protecting themselves."

"That would be logical. Should I have done something for myself?"

"No. I will take care of you."

She asked, "Do you have a goodly supply for this afternoon?"

He laughed.

"I have always heard this was the way to spend a rainy afternoon. Now, I understand why."

"I have found an insatiable woman?"

"Well, I would like a little more time, this time. Do not be in such a rush."

He was not. He was exquisitely slow. He took the rest of the afternoon, and no one disturbed them.

He took her along sensual trails she had never dreamed existed, and she went adventuresomely along, eagerly exploring. She set him on his ear.

When he took her that time, he was very gentle and careful. It was she who was impatient.

And when they rested again, she smiled and the sounds in her throat were like contented purrs.

Dominic knew he had found paradise. Not just in release, but actually. She was perfect.

Eight

They had their first quarrel as Fiona sought her clothing. "How did this get clear over here?" she exclaimed in English.

At first Dominic had intended helping her dress, but he was mesmerized by her beautifully nude body as she bent and straightened, and as she shook her clothing straight, she jiggled. He was enchanted, and sat on the bed to observe this magic woman. "Where are you going?" He smiled as he watched her.

In English, she replied, "I can't have anyone see me like this in your room. I must get back to my own."

"Why?"

She looked at him in some surprise that he would ask such a question but felt no need to explain it to a man of his age. She shook out her panties and turned them right-side out.

"Don't put those on. I like looking at you."

She put a hand on her hip and huffed. "Are you mad? If I stayed this way and was in your room, everyone would . . . know!" She bent over to pick up her blouse.

He smiled lazily. "They already know."

She jerked her head around and stared at him. "How could they?"

"They've watched me come home for lunch and come home to swim with you. They've heard me tell them to guard you. They know." His voice was complacent.

She straightened. "Good grief." She pinched her mouth up and frowned at him. "How could you do that, when I've been so careful."

He loved that. "Did you hide that you wanted to be with me?"

She turned her blouse right-side out. "I've been very circumspect."

Placidly, he lounged back on the bed, glorious in his nude, contented state, and he assured her, in Italian, "I have not."

She looked at him wide-eyed and indignant, and she spoke in English. "What do you mean?"

He was courteous and also spoke English. "From the time I saw you sleeping in my chair that first day, I have had you . . . staked out."

Her lips parted in amazement. She said, "The seal man."

He raised his eyebrows minutely in question, for she had lost him. Seal man?

She stepped into her panties, and he lost all thread of the conversation. How perfect she was. But then she pulled her blouse over her head and down to her hips. How awful to corrupt that body with clothes. He would take her away to an island and they would wear no clothes the entire time . . . until he had sated himself and lost his possessive interest in her. "I know of an island—"

"Do you know what time it is?" She looked at him in horror. "It's almost five. Where is Benjamin?"

That annoyed him. "They will care for Benjamin. Come here. I know of an island—"

She said starkly, "You just said . . . you said that 'they' will take care of Benjamin!"

"Yes. And you can take care of me." He smiled with all his boggling store of charm.

She wondered what was the name for a male siren who lured women? "But I am here to take my mother's place. 'Take care of Benjamin!' I was told that there was no one to care for Benjamin."

Impatiently, his hand brushed her words aside. Then he really understood that he had botched it. He said very carefully, "You are right. I forget Benjamin, now and then. I have been very busy. But you lured me with your relaxed sleeping figure. With your quick glances and your sassy tongue. I have wanted you since I saw you sleeping in my chair."

"But there was no real reason for me to stay here for Benjamin."

He was silent as he weighed how angry she might become as the reality of his ruse occurred to her.

She elaborated, "You said—"

"Not enough, obviously. I could not believe you were mortal. How could I know that you would come here, and that you would be perfect? I could think of nothing else—"

"But getting me into bed." She elaborated his premise.

"Onto the rug," he corrected teasingly, and he grinned, inviting her to laugh.

She was not amused. "I have a job. I need to go back to it."

"No!" He rolled up off that bed in the most thrilling display of male power and came to take her shoulders into his big hands.

She faltered. Her eyes were pleading. "I need to get away from here."

"Benjamin does need you." Dominic soothed her. "He's just a little boy. Stay. Stay."

"Oh, Dominic, what are you doing to me? I need to be away from you, so that I can think."

His eyes glittered with her words. "I shall think for you."

"No."

"I want you." His deep voice was thrilling. "I want you here with me."

She shook her head and tried to twist away. "You just want sex."

"That, too." He was earnest. "Fiona. Stay here with me. With Benjamin. Stay here where you belong."

"For now." She amended his words.

"You loved making love with me," he reminded her, and he used her English.

"You are skilled." She tilted her head back, to see his eyes. They were intense and seemed to bore into hers with command. She closed her own, in order to resist his lure.

"Stay here." His voice, then, was soft and sure.

And she hedged. "I have promised my mother I shall stay six more days. But you must keep your distance."

"Why?" He was indignant. "What difference would it make?"

"A lot. I'm not your live-in convenience."

That offended him, and he went back to Italian. "I have not treated you with disrespect. You wanted me. You know that. Why should you now punish us both? You loved with me. You liked me."

She followed him into his language. "This one time. Not again. I cannot explain how this happened. You know very well that I have never been with a man before I was with you. I am not that kind to sleep around."

He was a little arrogant. "And you have known that I am not a marrying man."

"You have had two wives to prove that?"

"No longer. Fiona—"

"No. I cannot."

He stood, magnificently naked, as he watched her finish dressing. That chore silently completed, she looked at him, and he was gratified that her glances went over his body.

She said, "Truly, Dominic, you are a great lover. In my small experience, no other man has tempted me. I do not regret our sharing."

That little speech scared him the most of all.

She went to her room to shower, weeping, and she changed clothing. She carefully applied makeup and finally had to wrap a bandage around her finger to explain her tear-mottled face. It unsettled her to anticipate seeing Dominic again, because she might fall to his feet and beg his pardon for rejecting his offered affair. Could she be so spineless? Probably.

Benjamin came upstairs, full of himself, carrying a kitten. "See? Fiona, I slept on the STRAW! And the kitten slept, too. See it? It's a baby cat! Like I'm a little boy." He grinned up at Fiona, full of new information she really did not hear.

Benjamin talked all through a bath and clothes change. And he carried the kitten down to supper. She dreaded going down and facing Dominic. How could she sit at the table with him and not cry and make a fool of herself?

But he'd left. His absence caused great despair in Fiona. That was a contradiction. She didn't want to see him and then, when he wasn't there, she became desolate.

Momma wouldn't allow the kitten on the table, and Benjamin questioned her right to deny him that. The men were no help. They were amused and entertained that the martinet had met her match. Fiona finally had to say to Benjamin, "Sit down and be quiet."

He did that.

Everyone was impressed, and Momma gave Fiona a studying look of respect. But Fiona did not notice. She was sunk into her misery.

The next three days were an endless desert of despair. Dominic was nowhere around. Fiona functioned. She walked through the days and did not notice the men's compassionate regard, or that even Momma was kind. Benjamin did not notice anything was wrong.

Then Romano came to Fiona, who was sitting on the porch. The continuing rain kept her and Benjamin prisoners under the roof. The kitten was a tiny purring ball on her lap, and Benjamin was working on something monstrous with his Lego set. He was warmly dressed, sitting on a thick rug that had been laid on the reed porch rug.

In an unusual move, Romano sat down and concentrated his attention on Fiona. She gradually realized that he wished to speak with her. She gave him reluctant, indifferent attention.

He said, "Lorenzo swims at night. It is forbidden."

Simple words. But they got Fiona's attention. They froze her dying soul.

So that night when Dominic came through the cold September drizzle into the house, carrying his wet clothing and towel, wearing only his swimming trunks, he found that Fiona waited for him. She was sitting at the bottom of the stairs and she was dressed.

He stopped at the first glimpse of her and stared as if she might well be a mirage there in his lower hall at that time of night, alone. He waited, as if she might vanish.

In terse English, she said angrily, "You have been swimming at night. It is forbidden."

She was upset with him. She was quarreling about his safety. She had said that he was not to swim at night? "Who says?" he questioned arrogantly in Italian.

"Lorenzo."

His name on her tongue had power over him, but he asked cynically, "Who is he?" If she cared nothing for him, he was nothing.

"He is a stubborn man." She shook her head slowly.

"But a human man. One who is sundered by an obstinate woman."

"Oh, Dominic..." And she began to weep. "Promise me that you will not swim at night. That you will not swim alone. Something horrible could happen to you."

She had betrayed herself.

He dropped his towel and dripping clothing to the floor and went to her. He took her hand and coaxed her to rise. That was her last chance to demur.

She stood up in surrender and he kissed her, holding her to his heating body. He lifted his mouth and said, "Oh, Fiona." Then he scooped her into his arms and carried her up the stairs to his room.

And she gave up. She wept as he undressed her, but she kissed him back and her hands caressed him. She helped him take away her clothing, and she welcomed him to her with small sounds of need.

She spent the night in his bed. In his arms. In love. Their loving was very serious, very tender. It was exquisitely done and deeply moving, as deep as his thrusts, as moving as her sighs sounded to his ears. As exquisite as their passionately shared rapture.

By morning she knew she would stay as long as he would allow her to be with him. That was sobering. He was very possessive of her. He held her. Even sated, he touched her. And when he said "You won't leave me," she already knew that was so.

With daylight, Dominic left their bed. He was gone when she wakened to stretch tired muscles and to find him gone. But she knew that he would return to her... for now.

Her body had been well used. It was replete and a little sore. She smiled shyly and blushed, as she trailed from his room, down the hall and into her own room to shower and dress. Then she wakened Benjamin. He chatted about something or other, and they went down to breakfast.

At the bottom of the steps, she recalled last night's initial encounter. She saw that some time during the night, one of the prowling shadows must have picked up Dominic's wet towel and clothes and carried them away. And someone must have wiped up the puddles, for there was no evidence that Dominic had so carelessly come into the house.

He came home in the middle of the day and had lunch with the cheerful watching men and an attentive Momma. He sat by Fiona, and made no bones about his attention to her. She was one continuous blush.

Alex did say that he was taking Benjamin to the barn again. And everyone vanished, even Momma. The two were alone. If they had been paying any attention to anything besides each other, they could have readily suspected a conspiracy. But they simply thought that since they were acting ordinarily, so was everyone else. The lovers expected the staff to be busy, and they expected to be left alone because they chose to be.

Dominic took Fiona up to his room, and she went willingly, laughing softly. He had brought her a bracelet. He said, "I have this for you." And he showed her the fragile golden bracelet on his hard palm. She started to take it from his hand, but he closed his fingers around it. "It is for your ankle," he said in Italian.

His words gave her a strange feeling. For an independent second-generation liberated woman, the thought of wearing an ankle bracelet was jarring. Those were called slave bracelets.

She watched quite soberly as he put it on her ankle, took out several of the golden links, fastened it into place, then took a snub-nosed pair of pliers and smashed the clasp so that it could not be removed.

She curled her leg up and looked at the engraving on the golden tag centered in the links of gold. It read, *She Is Mine. D.L.*

She looked up at him and asked in a serious voice, "How many other women wear your bracelets?"

"None. I never felt the need to mark a woman as my own."

"I am considered an independent woman. My mother brought me up as a liberated woman. I have convictions that go counter to slave bracelets." She said that as she sat there with an unremovable one on her ankle.

"You are free to do anything you choose to do." He was very open about it. "Except that you may not leave me, you must sleep in my bed and you may not look at another man."

"You're closing me in. You're asking me to live in sin."

She shocked him. "What we share is not sinful. We are committed to each other."

"For now." She watched him.

He faltered and moved uncomfortably, but he did not clarify that and he could not deny it. So he avoided saying anything concerning serious commitment. Instead, he said, "Do you like my gift?"

"I am not sure."

"You will wear it?" He pressed for her reply.

"I cannot take it off." She could break the chain. She had admitted that she would not.

He made love to her. He did it with such relish. He sampled her and tempted her, and he loved her marvelously. Then he took her. He did that wondrously, thrilling her and giving her exquisite pleasure. But he did not say any words of love.

However, when they were replete, he moved down her body, kissing here and there in small salutes, until he knelt below her feet. There, he circled his hand around her ankle on the bracelet as he lifted her foot to his chest. Then looking up her body to her face, he leaned down and kissed the bracelet. It was a thrilling happening. He had done it so deliberately, that it was meaningful to him. What did he mean by it?

During the days that followed, she would recall his act and wonder, but she did not have the courage to ask him what he had meant by such a...ceremony. For it had been that.

Dominic took Fiona to see the winter house. It was a jewel. It, too, was on the shores of Lake Michigan, but at Winnetka.

The house was of Italian marble, but it looked deceptively small and delicate. That was what surprised Fiona. She had expected a man's strong house. She asked, "Have all your wives lived here?"

"I have had two. Neither lived here." He gave her a droll look of reproof, but she ignored him.

He showed her the rooms where the "family" lived. He showed her the formal ones, with beautiful furnishings and lovely paintings.

She indicated the paintings. "Where did you find these?"

"In traveling."

"Do you travel much?" She frowned, for she would miss being with him.

"You will go with me."

He took her to his quarters and made love to her there on his bed. "The house must know you are in charge."

"In charge? Over Momma? You jest."

"It is so." He said that sternly.

"Do not tell her or she will intimidate me."

That only made Dominic laugh.

The last of the ten days of promise went by without verbal notice. Fiona's mother had been released from the hospital and was again at the Evanses' home where she had around-the-clock attendants.

Maria was in physical therapy and progressing well. And when Fiona saw her mother and noted her determined progress, there was a flutter in Fiona's stomach. In the spring, her mother would return to Benjamin. There would no longer be any legitimate excuse for Fiona to be at the compound. What would happen to Fiona?

Finally, Fiona went to see Kevin McBride and resigned from her job. He was sentimental about losing her, but it was just friendship. He had hired Angelina, and he smiled at her in the way that he used to smile at Fiona. That gave Fiona a nostalgic pang.

Angelina told Fiona, "The best thing you ever did for me was bringing me in here. I adore Kevin. I am making him dangle, so that he'll be so glad when I accept him—that I will be able to do no wrong in his eyes. It's a stupid woman who allows a man to rule her."

It was a stupid, sobered woman who occupied Fiona's body as she drove slowly back to the compound...with Nick.

The staff was getting ready for the move to the winter home. Momma was shouting and directing, so

Fiona took Benjamin and went to the library. Nick was relieved to go along and get away from the tyrant who was Momma.

Fiona wasn't even included in the duties of the move. She felt left out, as unimportant as a fifth wheel. She had no place, no duties, no responsibilities. She was Dominic's woman. That was all.

So the move was completed, and they were established in the winter house. The daily routine was very similar to that in the summer house.

To Fiona, Maria had firmly set out the idea of a compound preschool for the children of the people who lived there, and perhaps some of the other family offspring. Benjamin needed more interplay with other children.

Fiona presented the idea to Dominic by degrees. She pointed out that Benjamin was in control of the entire household staff. It was not good for a child to have that power. He needed the give-and-take of other children. A school would be the solution.

Dominic took the idea calmly and said he would think on it.

Fiona's family was invited to the compound for dinner almost right away. They were not terribly impressed. Evans was an English name, and English stock was never impressed. The Garibaldis went back generations to wealth long-lost, but it was still genetically remembered, and they had become used to their current affluence.

Her papa asked, "Where is your room?"

The lovers had anticipated just such a question, and Fiona took her father to see her room near Benjamin's. She had possessions there, and her knitting was by a window chair. The room looked occupied.

And her papa asked, "Does he behave? He looks like a predator."

She lied, "He is a gentleman."

"Don't give him an inch. He's the kind that takes everything."

That just showed her papa knew about men such as Dominic.

With the cold weather, and the glorious fall-colored trees, Dominic began to spend more of the daytime at home while he continued to work late into the night. With Benjamin and Fiona, he tramped the shoreline and watched the flyways of ducks and geese going south. Benjamin was enthralled. "Far away."

Dominic said, "Yes. Some go to Texas and some go clear down to South America."

That meant nothing to Benjamin. Nor did the instruction on the world globe in the library. Then Benjamin said, "High." And they understood his "far away" had meant up into the air from his place on the ground.

As the weather worsened there on the lake, Dominic lounged inside with them, and he read aloud to them from the newspapers or from magazine articles. He did not read children's books or play children's games, but he spent more time with Benjamin. They became friends, and Dominic demanded and got Benjamin's obedience. He and Fiona were the only two who were not cripplingly indulgent to the darling little boy. And Dominic entertained the idea of a compound school in a kinder way.

Dominic took Benjamin to the ice rink and began to teach him how to ice-skate. Fiona was amazed. "Do they ice-skate in Italy?"

Dominic laughed. "I do not know. But Italians in Chicago do."

It was a lazy time filled with activity. Dominic watched the winter games on television, and he made delicious, inventive love to Fiona. Several times, in the throes of their love, she whispered shyly that she loved him; and he groaned, holding her tightly, temporarily stunned by his own answering emotion.

She learned to go to bed early in her own room and waken when Dominic returned near midnight. At a counter in his suite, there were the means to prepare or heat snacks. She always had some light treat for him, and she would sit with him as he paced and nibbled while he gestured and talked.

She would knit as he told her of his successes, of the people he met and why they acted as they did. She admired him, and he basked in her praise, moving rather arrogantly and smiling in his pleasure at her attention.

She wondered if no one had ever listened to him before then.

He gave her an allowance that she would not touch. She frustrated him. He opened a bank account and checking account, and the checks lay unused. He would open her desk and look at them, still pristine. He would be angry. But she would not use his money.

The Lorenzo compound did celebrate Thanksgiving, and the Evanses came to that meal. Together, the combined families were all a big, noisy bunch, with children exploring and with much talk and laughter and a few salty quarrels . . . but those were not among the Evanses.

At Christmastime, there was the excitement of shopping and secrets, the choosing of the tree and decorating it. There was the baking of cookies and allowing a little boy to get half-sick with licking the icing from the bowls and helping.

Fiona had knitted Dominic a sweater, which he admired carefully and wore in a strutting way that melted her completely.

And he gave Fiona a fantastic diamond necklace with matching earrings and bracelet that awed her and amazed her, but that she could not keep. He quarreled with her, and she did explain, but he could not understand such foolishness. He did use that word, and she was kind.

He would not speak to her for two days. He told her she was a Pilgrim. He again labeled her as foolish. She would not take back the diamonds. He bought her a house full of flowers and sprinkled their bed—and her body—with rose petals. Naked, she put on the earrings and he put the necklace on her. She told him, "You are a stubborn man."

He had heard that before.

And Nick became enamored with Fiona's sister. If they married, Philippa would know of Fiona's place in Dominic's life. And Fiona became quieter.

Dominic said to her, "You are a month early with your blahs. It is too soon for the February blues. You need to get out and do something like buy a new hat?"

"I think I would like to find a job."

That only made him cross. "That again. You have enough money, if you would use it. You don't need *another* job."

Her job was to be his companion and bed partner. She specified that. "For my own sake, I need to have some sort of face-saving work. I am a kept woman."

But he refused to discuss it. Worse, he forbade her getting a job.

She did go out. And it was then that, as they walked across a room in the library, the door of one of the listening cubicles opened, and Benjamin stopped dead in his tracks. He stood and listened intently. Then his face brightened and he became excited. He grabbed Fiona's skirt and said, "Mama! That's Mama!"

Fiona frowned at Benjamin. The woman's voice sounded nothing at all like Momma's. She said, "No, Benjamin..."

But he ran for the cubicle saying, "Mama?" His face was so eagerly expectant. He looked inside the empty room, puzzled. "Mama?"

"What is it, Benjamin?" Fiona's attention was captured.

He went carefully to the machine and touched it. "Mama." But he did not understand. He looked around the little room and then at the machine. Then he turned his little face up to Fiona and questioned, "Mama? Where is Mama?"

"The voice?" Fiona urged.

Benjamin nodded. "Mama reads my book."

The person came back to the cubicle and waited, watching.

Fiona said, "Whose voice is that?"

"Uh... Let's see." The woman found a sheaf of papers and went down it. "She's a volunteer reader. We don't give out names."

"Is she a mother?"

"Not that I know. She's not married."

"Could we buy a copy of the tape?"

"Yes," said the volunteer. "I'm making up some now."

Puzzled, searching, Benjamin asked, "Where is Mama?" The woman asked what was wrong? And Fiona explained that the tape sounded like the voice of the boy's mother.

When the tape was finished, they picked it up at the desk. Benjamin had listened carefully to Fiona's explanation of the tape, but she knew he did not necessarily understand her. He insisted on carrying the package. They went home, and Fiona was very quiet.

That night she got the tape from Benjamin's machine and carried it to Dominic's room. After Dominic had come home, Fiona sat with him while he consumed the snacks that she had made for him. As he sat back with a contented sigh, she asked, "Who was Benjamin's mother? You mentioned that she was from Texas?"

"Yes. Why?"

"Her name was different. What was it?"

"Tate." His reply was short.

"She never contacts you or Benjamin. Did she abandon him?"

"Why do you ask this of me?"

"We have spoken once or twice of how long little children remember things. Your son had an interesting experience today." And she told Dominic about the incident at the library.

He listened stonily, but he made no comment.

Fiona went to the tape machine and put in the tape. She turned it on low, and they listened to the voice of the woman.

"That's enough. I don't find children's stories engrossing."

"Is that Tate's voice?"

"I don't remember."

Nine

Fiona's voice was mild and completely reasonable. "How can you *not* remember?" she asked Dominic. "She was your wife. You lived together... two years? Three?"

"Two." Dominic replied so coldly that icicles hung from his words. He scowled, wanting to be free of that defeat. "I have erased her memory."

Fiona lowered her eyelids to hide the disbelief that flared there. "How clever of you."

He looked at her sharply, but her face was serene. He was jarred by her confrontation and it rattled him. Restlessly awkward, he paced several times before he went to her. He lifted her, then carried her over and put her into his own chair. The chair had been brought over from the summer house because it was his. He stood and looked down at her.

Her long hair was freed from its knot and down around her shoulders. Her blue-green gaze was resting on his face with a tenderness that soaked into his bones. Her night robe was loose around her, and her cleavage was sweet to him, indicating the soft secrets still concealed.

He knelt down beside her and worked his arms around her hips to pull her body against his face as he had wanted to do that first time he saw her sleeping in his chair. "I saw you first, in this chair. I wanted to hold you, then, as I am holding you now. I had to clench my hands to keep from doing it then. I love you, Fiona." He heard her shivered gasp. "Marry me."

She took a quick breath of surprise, then she laughed a small, watery sound and chided, "Oh, Dominic, you're so stubborn. You're supposed to ask a lady to marry you, you're not supposed to tell her to do it."

He pulled back enough to look at her. His eyes were bloodshot with tears. In English, he told her, "I'm afraid. I'm a two-time loser."

In Italian, she scolded gently, "How could you be afraid of me? I love you with my very being. I could not harm you."

"Marry me?" He never quit looking into her eyes.

"Yes." She could not tease or delay, even though she was completely surprised and felt off-balance. She had resigned herself to being his woman for the rest of her life, on the edge of his.

"I can't have you feel . . . tarnished."

Her voice wavered. "I would do anything for you."

"Marry me. Don't ever leave me."

"Oh, Dominic, yes, yes, yes. And no, I won't ever leave you."

Their kiss was probably the most amateurish they had ever exchanged. She was weepy and disorganized, and he was not much better. Then he released her reluctantly, but in order to take a box from his pocket. The rock of a ring he took from the box was unbelievable.

With the ring, Fiona realized that he had planned the proposal. It had not been an impulse.

He put it on her finger, and she looked at it in astonishment. "My shoulder will slope wrong," she protested, making her left shoulder sag.

He almost smiled. "I'll buy you another for balance."

"Then my back will bend from the carat weight." And she laughed. She held her hand up and admired the ring. She exclaimed, "I could sit on the front of a train and replace the headlight with my hand and the ring would light the way for it."

In Italian, he told her, "I would cover you with gems and rings and golden things."

Very seriously, she put her hands on either side of his face to look into his eyes, as she replied in that language, "I would have only you to cover me."

Their kisses, then, were profound. He was secure for the first time with her, and his passion was free and exuberant. He loved her with no more self-doubt, no more restraints to himself. His touches were different, more possessive, more confident. And his words of love were beautiful.

The next day there was great jubilation on the compound. And later on that day, they made a formal call on Fiona's parents. Her mother's lack of astonishment gave Fiona some distracted pause, but her attention was caught by her father, who said, "You must move back home immediately, today."

Dominic went very still.

"Papa?" Fiona ventured that.

He stood up. This was serious. "A woman must be married from her own home. It would not look right if you stayed in the house of your intended. People would talk."

"But, Papa—"

In English, Dominic said sternly, "He is right."

Fiona gasped and stared at Dominic. He was unmovable. She looked, then, at her Italian mother, knowing there was no hope there.

Maria Garibaldi Evans smiled. "Come home, little one, and we prepare for the wedding together. Everyone will come."

But this time it was Dominic who lifted a quieting hand. "I cannot have a big wedding. I have carefully guarded my anonymity. I wear the cloak of grain supplier. My interests are greater than that. My dealings are legitimate. I am an honorable man, but I could become too newsworthy. I do not want to become a public man. The wedding must be quietly limited to the immediate families."

He looked at Fiona. "I am sorry, my love. We would lose the little freedom we now have. But your father is right that you must move back here for now. Benjamin will miss you." And his tender smile did not need words to say that so would he.

It was then Fiona found that Dominic used d'Angelo as a public last name. And she discovered that her parents had both known that.

Then, Dominic asked for an appointment with his father-in-law-to-be.

Ned opened his arms out. "Appointment? I'm free now. What is it? You need a loan." He was being droll, but his shrewd eyes weighed Dominic.

They moved aside, in the little Evans house, to another room, so that they could discuss their business.

"No." Dominic, too, smiled. "No loan. We need to discuss a marriage settlement, and a prenuptial agreement."

Ned said, "She doesn't have a dowry. All our jewels are children."

"My settlement to you is for your daughter."

"You're *buying* her?" He was somewhat belligerent under his astonishment.

Dominic was trying to live by the old rules. He explained, "You will give her to me."

Ned told the younger man, "You don't know Maria Garibaldi's daughters. They are new women. They don't go by the old rules. You don't owe us anything. You've taken care of all those hospital bills, and even those here at home. Maria has had great care, because of you. We are indebted to you with our gratitude. But you don't get Fiona in payment. You get her because she's willing."

Dominic smiled at his father-in-law-to-be and kissed his cheeks with great dignity. Ned held still for it. He had watched that conduct with Maria's family. Now, the embrace touched his heart. He patted Dominic's shoulder and said, "You'll do." Then he blew his nose and shook his head, but he smiled.

Dominic gave Ned a list of the proposals, and that of the prenuptial agreement. "For Fiona, ask a lawyer that you would trust to look these over. We will meet to agree or negotiate. Fiona should be involved in this, so that she is content with the arrangements. Please do this. I ask it of you."

"I will read them and give you my opinion."

"You get a lawyer to look at them." Dominic was firm.

"Yes. Okay. There is no need. If I didn't trust you, Maria wouldn't have worked at your compound and Fiona wouldn't have gone there, either."

Dominic didn't give up. "A lawyer. On your word. I wish to do this."

"I said, okay."

As they moved slowly back to rejoin the rest of the family, Dominic told Ned, "My men say that you would make a good Italian. From them, that's a high compliment."

"I accept that as such, but it's a good thing I'm not. I'm good, solid English stock. I'm all that keeps Maria anchored. She's like a kite in a strong wind, and I'm her string to the solid ground. She flies, but she has me to keep her reasonably controlled."

Dominic laughed out loud.

"What's so funny?" Fiona came to Dominic and put her hand through his arm to press it to her discreetly. Her face was radiant and her eyes sparkled.

"Your father declines to be an Italian."

"I know." Fiona grinned. "The Garibaldis tried, but the Evanses are staunchly supportive of him staying an Evans."

"Which are you?" Dominic inquired.

"Probably mostly Evans. Level, staunch and very loyal."

"And emotional." Her father added that, with sentiment.

"But not volatile," her mother added with a wavering smile.

Fiona gave Dominic a precious look and summed it up. "I'm darling."

He hugged her hand against his body, and apologized, "I have no family to recommend me so well."

And Maria said, staunchly Italian, "I recommend you. You are a good man."

"Stubborn," corrected Fiona.

And before her parents, Dominic said to Fiona, "I am a man who loves you and who will cherish you." Then he looked at Ned. "May I marry your daughter?"

Ned smiled and opened his mouth, but it was Maria who said, "Yes."

When the lovers met, it was as if they had been weeks apart instead of meeting just yesterday. Fiona still went to the winter compound each day to be with Benjamin. She wore that rock of a ring. And everyone smiled at her.

They explained the marriage to Benjamin, because he wanted to know why she was not there in the night. With the careful choosing and remembering of words to communicate, he told her, "I miss you. I get up and go to your room, and you're not there."

"What do you do?" Fiona asked him.

"I go to Papa."

"Good."

His eyes searching around, he elaborated. "Papa reads me...business reports. I go to sleep." He sighed.

And Fiona laughed.

The boy asked earnestly, "How soon will you come home?"

"Soon."

Finally Valentine's Day did come, and the day of the wedding. The two families and several choice, outside inclusions gathered for the simple ceremony, and Dominic and Fiona were married.

Fiona wore a long-skirted, long-sleeved white silken gown that was simple and beautiful. On her head she wore a crown of flowers and ribbons. She looked so beautiful that everyone was touched with sentimental tears.

It was all so easy. It was such fun. There were no major hang-ups or mistakes. Benjamin was delighted with all of the children who attended. It was as if he had been suddenly mixed in with his own kind. He was included, which was wonderful. Children can be slow to accept a stranger. And he had a great time with just people.

Fiona watched him, monitoring him that he was not too tired or that they were all behaving properly, and she thought of his mother. His mother never saw him like this, his face flushed in laughter, his darling body and hands. What sort of woman was that Tate that she shunned her child?

But the party went on, and Fiona was distracted by family stories that Dominic must hear, and she needed to protest, "No, no, no! Not that!" And they laughed and told it anyway. Dominic would look at her and smile.

The food was excessive. Having a laden table with the dishes of the family favorites of both nationalities led to gluttony, one of the seven deadly sins. The strange thing was that even the pudding had an Italian accent.

There had been nothing in the papers other than the usual license listing, and even there, Dominic was listed as d'Angelo.

But Angelina knew of the wedding, and Kevin sent a bouquet.

Dominic could not take his glances, his intent regard from Fiona, and she loved it. She blushed and laughed and held his hand. He could not believe that she was now his wife. She was truly his.

But he remembered his other marriages, both of which had begun with similar feelings. He had never felt this particular commitment to either of his other wives. He had been blind with possessive lust for his first wife, and bemused by the exuberant, adventuresome curiosity of his second. It was only now that he entered marriage with the commitment of love and nurturing of a mate.

Did she feel that way? Did she love him...enough? Would this marriage work? Fiona had never mentioned the prenuptial agreement or its generous settlements if they divorced. His lawyers had been appalled by his insistence on his terms. "She'll divorce you the second week and be set for life!"

Would she?

Angelina caught the bouquet. But Kevin was not there to see it. He had not been included on the meager guest list. Angelina had explained to Kevin that Fiona was marrying a very private man.

The newlyweds drank very little of the wine. Their hands touched, and if they were moved apart by talking, gesturing members of the families, the lovers' gazes locked and she smiled. He was serious.

Fiona's mother and father had insisted that Benjamin spend the wedding night with them and myriad new cousins and discreet Lorenzo guards. It would be Benjamin's first slumber party, and he was so excited and laughed so much that he was asleep before it began. Fiona looked on him, sleeping, such a beautiful child. She wondered at the woman who had been his mother.

It was late when, at last, the newlyweds returned to the guarded compound and went to their own suite of rooms.

Dominic called Fiona Mrs. Lorenzo, as most newly married men label their wives, as such, by using their new name. And so she called him Mr. Lorenzo. Her blushes continued, as did her smiles. She was truly a new bride. Why was she shy with him? They were not strangers.

"Take down your hair," he asked. "Don't braid it tonight."

"You don't mind getting tangled in it?"

"You can tangle any of me in it that you choose."

He removed her crown of flowers and ribbons to lay it aside. Then he watched her shake out her hair and take off her clothing. She was beautiful in the minimal light of their room.

He removed his own clothing, conscious that she observed him with a pleasure of her own, and he moved to display his body to her.

Without his clothes, he went to her and took her against him, to feel the wonder of her soft body with his own hard surfaces. And he thought that women could never know what it was like to the men who were allowed to hold them, the magical difference.

He said, "Are you ready for bed, Mrs. Lorenzo?"

And she blushed yet again. "Yes."

"Why are you shy with me?"

"I don't know. It's only that this is a ceremony that means I can sleep with you properly."

"Oh? Is there an improper way to do that, Mrs. Lorenzo?"

"Sometime I may demonstrate what I've heard along that line."

"Not now?"

She shook her head. "This is too serious."

As they crawled naked into their bed, Fiona said, "There are some other things to which you must agree."

His jaw hardened. Here it came. She wanted more money. He had paused in pulling up the blanket. His voice was a little grim as he asked, "What." And he knew with some self-disgust that whatever she requested, he would probably give it to her.

"In winter, you have to warm my cold feet. That includes some summer storms, when it becomes unseasonably cool."

"I can do that." He lay down and reached for her feet, pulling them up along his hip, holding them in his hot hands.

She said "Umm," with pleasure. Then she told him, "You have to rub my back when I'm pregnant." She had listed another demand.

"Yes."

"You must listen to me when I need to speak about something."

He put her feet over his hip and pulled her closer. "I will listen."

"Cheerfully." She pulled back to look at his serious face as she amended the rule.

He repeated, "Cheerfully."

"And you must not scold me if I'm sentimental."

"I will not." He was still. Then he asked, "And?" as he waited for the crux of the demands.

"That's all." She wiggled closer. "Except that I would like you to hold me and to kiss me mindless and maybe even have legitimate sex with me."

"You want nothing else of me?" He could not believe she was not going to hold him up for some outrageous promise. Women did that.

"That's all."

"And you want nothing more?"

"Well, I don't want you to fill my request to hug me and love me and have sex with me just tonight. I expect you to continue fooling around with me for all the rest of our long, long lives."

"Yes." He did not move, so she kissed under his chin. He asked, "Did you see the prenuptial agreements?"

"We didn't need that. You're married to me for life. Rich or poor, in sickness or in health, the whole oath."

"Yes." His voice trembled, and he said, "Oh, Fiona..."

"I'm so glad you married me. I really thought I'd spend my life just being your woman of convenience."

With some emotion, he said, "No." And he began to think that perhaps she loved him truly.

She rubbed her hand down his chest and flicked his nipple with a fingernail. "It would be nice if you told me that you love me."

He kissed her until she was melting. In Italian, he said, "I love you." He said, "My wife." And he said, "Let me give you a baby."

Blushing, smiling, she nodded.

He said, "Do you understand what I have asked?"

"We've had our honeymoon," she said. "I would like to start our first baby."

And he was thrilled. Benjamin had been a fact before Dominic had married the second time. This was his third time in a marriage bed. And Fiona could be the most precious possession he had ever had. Possession? It was she who possessed him. He was her slave. She must not know that she could have anything she wanted of him. "You don't want to wait for a while to be pregnant?"

She touched her mouth to his and spoke as she flowered her lips to elaborately brush his. "No."

So, with their lives met, and with that purpose, their lovemaking was different, yet again. It was a marriage rite. It was not just body hunger or even just love. It was more than that. It was a scary thrill beyond what they had experienced, for it was commitment of another kind.

His hands on her body were different. There was knowledge in their touch, that they had embarked on a very serious determination. They would bring a child into the world for whom they would be responsible. It would be a deliberate choice.

And Dominic found that he loved that not-yet-conceived child. But he loved the vessel more. He kissed Fiona, and his voice was rough with his emotion. "My love."

"I feel a little scared. Will the baby want this life? What will it be? Do you care?"

"Healthy."

"Yes," she agreed. "We can be careful of that. Protect it."

"It will thrill me to put my seed into you without the barrier."

"I'm glad you cared about me enough not to risk us getting pregnant before now."

"I want to care for you, Fiona. I love you. I will love your babies and know them. It won't be as it has been with Benjamin. You gave him to me. I only watched over him. He didn't know me until you came here."

"He loves you."

"Yes." Dominic's voice was soft.

"So this will be our second child."

"Yes." Then he made sweet and tender love to her. And they panted to completion. Then lying lax, he told her very gently, "We may not make the baby this first time." His tone was cautioning. "But it will give me great pleasure to persevere."

"You lecher."

He demurred. "Only a dedicated man."

"How do you go about this process?" she asked in a wide-eyed voice. She elaborated. "This ... making of a baby? An older woman of eight once told me—as a younger, ignorant child—that babies were born through the tummy button. Is that how they are planted, too?"

"They aren't born that way." He adopted a droning, explaining voice. "They are born through the same channel through which they are planted. It is here."

"There? How illogical."

Still in that voice, he instructed, "Actually, it is more comfortable through that channel than through the navel. Did you know that babies born through the navel join the navy?"

"What a lot of tummy-button babies! So Frances was right?"

"Partly. But even those babies are planted through the channel I have indicated."

"Show me."

He showed her many things, as he explained along the way. He explained and demonstrated to such an extent that he not only aroused her passion again, but he about drove her crazy.

She panted at one time, "This process takes a long, tense time."

"I am trying to instruct you thoroughly."

"How about getting me thoroughly pregnant?"

And he buckled down to business. He slid into her welcoming body to be grasped with long legs wound around him, and then he appeared earnestly to try to get away. He worked at that vigorously, insidiously, marvelously. He changed strokes and she slid and moved and encouraged and begged.

He paused, their hot sweat intermingling, their bodies so sensitized that any touch sent shivers up and down their entire nervous system. They panted. He kissed her very seriously, so seriously and so sweetly that tears came to her eyes as they vowed their love. Then he carried them to the peak, and their climax was exquisite.

Still coupled, they lay silent. For once, Dominic did not have to get up again to discard the condom. They gently moved their hands on one another, just to touch the other. Their breathing slowed. Dominic adjusted them so that his weight was minimized and gradually they eased into the great peace that awaited them, and they slept.

They had shifted and turned, separating, hardly wakening, but they still lay crowded together in that great bed. He wakened to find her. He needed so little sleep. He leaned on an elbow and watched her sleep with such concentration of love that she opened her eyes, instantly conscious of where she was. And she smiled.

Serious-faced, he lifted his big, rough hand to smooth her hair away from her face. "I didn't get tangled in it."

So she pressed him back in the bed and she tangled her hair around and about him as she made love to him. She had never been so bold, and he was riveted. "Was this also Frances who told you this?"

"No. It was you."

"I never told you to do that." He was scandalized with delight.

"You did it to me."

"A nice Italian boy like me, did that?"

"Yes."

"Sh-sh-shocking," he said, drawing air through his teeth, lying rigid and very interested.

And she had her wily way with him.

He probably slept more that night than he had in twenty years. But she had exhausted him. When daylight came, they were both sleeping. When hadn't Dominic watched the sun rise or the fogged or cloudy day lighten? He slept. Contented, with his wife snuggled close to him, he slept.

When they finally wakened, they stretched and smiled at each other, to kiss gently. He allowed her to leave the bed, because he was embarrassed that he had been so greedy in the night and that he wanted her again. But he went in and watched her bathe. Then he helped her. And soon they were back in bed.

After he was quickly satisfied, she mentioned to him that, "I believe you like sex without using a condom."

"You are mine. I don't have to be a beggar with you, pleasing you so that I may make love to you. I can have you as I choose."

"I believe I heard you correctly."

"I only say it once."

"You're saying that now you can jump me any time?"

"You object?"

She laughed. "You are an arrogant, smug man."

"A satisfied man."

"Will that last long enough for me to have breakfast?"

"I don't believe I ever asked if you can cook."

"Oh," she said elaborately, "did you marry me to cook for you?"

"Not altogether," he explained. "But it would help if you can cook me a couple of eggs today, since the staff is carefully giving us time alone together."

She inquired, "Is that why it's so quiet?"

"Yes."

"We are completely alone?"

"Inside the house."

"Then it wouldn't ruin your macho image to fetch me breakfast in bed. I've had a hard night."

He laughed and leaned down to kiss her yet again. Her lips were red and her face was abraded by his beard. He touched her cheek. "Poor little bride of a hungry man."

"What sort of hunger?" she asked sassily.

"You know it well, by now."

"Let's try the eggs." She sat up and grimaced.

"Have I hurt you?"

"No. Just a little tender. I think I sprung my hip that last time."

"But you . . . you aren't hurt?"

"No. I can outlast you any time."

She made him laugh. "Come, woman, find me something to eat."

In the kitchen, they organized their breakfast. To her surprise, Dominic helped. He set the table. He made the toast. He found napkins.

They stuffed themselves. They had been too distracted to eat at their wedding. Now they made up for it. She said, "I love you, Dominic Lorenzo."

"I am glad," he replied. "It wouldn't be as much fun for you, if you were here without your consent. I am glad you were willing."

She gave him a patient look. "I was ready to marry you almost right away."

"You sniped and sassed and flouted my authority. You weren't sweet and smiling."

"I wanted you."

"You might have said something about that sooner. I didn't know you loved me until you were angry about my swimming alone at night."

"Don't you ever do that again."

"Don't shun me."

"Why would I ever do that?"

"We might not agree on something, and you would become angry."

"I could never really be angry with you, Dominic."

He looked at her and smiled.

She retorted, "I wear your slave bracelet. What power could a slave have over a master?"

"All power." And he kissed her. He believed that she could ask anything of him, and he would willingly comply.

Ten

Being married to Dominic Lorenzo revealed another world to Fiona. As the wife of this private man, she, too, used the d'Angelo name. She had charge accounts, savings and checking accounts, all under Fiona Evans d'Angelo. It was either that or get the cash from Dominic.

And she found that no mail was delivered to the compound. The middle of March, Fiona had started watching for the mailman, until she realized there was no mailbox. "No mailbox?" she asked Romano.

"We have a post-office box. One of the men goes for the mail. We rarely have any."

"Has anyone gone today?" she asked.

Romano replied, "No."

"Would you ask someone to check the box?"

Romano explained kindly, "We do that on Friday."

"I can go. Give me the key."

But he "forgot" the key, and that night Dominic asked Fiona, "Are you expecting a letter?"

"What's this about the post-office box? Why all the sweat over it?"

In Italian, Dominic replied, "No one is perspiring. Do you want your own key to the box? Who is writing to you? We need to know your contacts to screen them."

She sighed impatiently. "Benjamin's birthday is in three days."

"Is it?"

"You know that." She faked elaborate patience. "The first day of spring. I bought our presents for him. Is there something particularly you'd like to get him?"

He smiled at his love. She was almost two weeks past her period. He suggested, "A baby."

Fiona laughed. "I must be pregnant. Momma says for me to help feed Benjamin's growing cat, but I can't stand to smell the cat food. I can't drink coffee. Momma smiles."

"Did you explain that I have been diligent?"

"No-o-o." She blushed scarlet.

"I will get you a key for the box at the post office. Why, here is one in my pocket!" He appeared amazed. "I wished, and it appeared."

"You silly."

He didn't flinch at her label but he did briefly squint.

So every day, Fiona went to the branch post office that served their area, and there was no mail. Benjamin's birthday came, with a rattling party of the compound children and the recently acquired little cousins. The kids were exuberant and the adults exhausted.

Benjamin said, in satisfaction, "Good party. I like being four years old."

"Four." Dominic shook his head, and without his permission his mind sneaked back to the time that Benjamin had been two years old.

Fiona said to Benjamin, "We need to mark your height, so that you can see how much you grow between now and when you are five."

Fiona was especially tender with Benjamin, because he was four years old and his mother had not contacted him, not even with a printed birthday card. Then, as she went to check on the boy before going to her own bed, she heard the taped story, which Benjamin thought was his mother reading to him. That brought tears to Fiona's eyes.

When she got up groggily to be with Dominic as he came home from the office at midnight, Fiona thought again of the hard-hearted woman who could ignore her child's birthday.

Dominic came in, his coat cold from the brisk spring air, and he scolded her. "Wait until I take it off. I will chill you."

She smiled and flung herself into his arms, not able to wait long enough for him to take off his coat. He held her tightly while he pulled the coat aside and brought Fiona against his heat. Then he wrapped his coat around her, too, and they stood, kissing.

As Dominic stripped out of his clothes and went to shower, Fiona took out a plate of nibbles and heated some of them. Wrapped in a robe, he returned to their room. He settled down with a pleased sound. Then

Fiona served him cranberry juice with the nibbles, and she replenished his plate.

"What is it?" he asked.

That surprised her. But even knowing that he would not want to discuss it, she did not brush it aside. "Is Tate dead?"

He was startled, shocked. "Why?"

"She didn't contact Benjamin for his birthday."

He did not respond.

"What kind of woman could be that aloof from so young a child?"

In all good, writhing conscience, Dominic said, "She would think of him."

There was a bleakness to his words. She studied her beloved. "She is dead?"

He hedged. "I haven't heard that."

So, then, Fiona assumed that little Benjamin was more than likely a half orphan. And he did remember his mother. Dominic had been so sure that the child would have forgotten her, but just her voice *in a strange place* had caught Benjamin's attention. Children do remember.

The Lorenzos' lives settled into a routine. Fiona was, indeed, pregnant. She told Dominic, "You should be a little embarrassed to have made me pregnant so easily. There are people who get to fool around for months and even years."

He cocked his dark, wickedly handsome head and looked at her from under those scandalous lashes as he smiled very salaciously.

She asked the ceiling, "Why am I surprised?"

At Maria Garibaldi Evans's instigation, Fiona had continued to urge Dominic to allow Benjamin and the other young children connected with the compound to be gathered into a nursery school three days a week. While Fiona had pushed for the school, Dominic had delayed. But Maria had continued to nudge for it.

And Fiona mentioned to Dominic, "Benjamin is lonely for other children."

"We are working on that," he replied complacently.

She gave him an elaborately patient look of disgust. "We should include the children of the men who work here," she explained. "It will help the wives. But it will help Benjamin most of all. I am concerned for him."

He said thoughtlessly, "You are not his mother."

She was jolted by his words, but she lowered her head and said furiously, "I am all he has."

"My God, Fiona, how could I have said that to you?"

"You blurted an honest opinion. I accept it. But I am on his side. To raise him as the only child among adults will harm him."

"You may organize the school." His voice was reluctant. Then he added, "Perhaps some of the Evanses and Garibaldis would be interested. There would be no charge."

"No. We will charge what they would pay for a sitter." Then she had the gall to add, "The men here need better salaries."

"They have good salaries," Dominic huffed. "What would they do without me?"

And coldly she asked, "What would you do without them?"

He made no reply.

So she instructed him further. "Money is only money. Don't be so strict with yours. Spread it around."

"I am building a kingdom for Benjamin and the new baby."

"They won't want kingdoms. They will want friends."

"You are interfering."

She enunciated. "Quite possibly."

Darkly somber, he watched her. But she patted her stomach and burped. Her food did not sit well those days. And his heart melted. She was right. But he did not tell her that. He just walked around restlessly, not leaving the room, and he scuffed his feet some to call her attention to himself. He waited for her to say something, so that he could be gracious in replying.

She looked at her watch. "I'm due at the library. I probably won't see you until you come home tonight."

"Let Nick drive you."

She retorted, very patiently, "We've talked that to death."

"I worry for you."

She said in smug English, "I can handle anything."

He warned, "Not me." Then he tilted his head back and smiled just a bit.

"If I tried, I might even handle you."

He grinned. "I am more than you think. You would be pinned in no time."

She sighed gustily. "That again." Then she said saucily, "There is no need to 'pin' me. I am already pregnant."

In Italian, he elaborated. "We practice for the next one."

"Ahh. I hadn't realized that you would need practice, such a man as skilled as you."

"I need to hone my methods."

"Perhaps you will explain this 'honing' to me?"

"Count on it."

At the library, who should Fiona see but Finnig! For a man who looked as if he were braced against an unknown attacker, the library seemed an odd place for him to be.

He nodded gravely.

Fiona asked, "Why are you here?"

And he replied quite well, really. He said, "I'm learning to talk—to say things better."

"You're doing very well."

He nodded once, to acknowledge what she had said. "Are you okay?" Finnig chose his words almost as carefully as Benjamin. He said, "Kevin will ask if I have seen you. He says you are married to a man named d'Angelo. Does he treat you okay...all right?"

"Tell Kevin all is well."

"I will."

So that night she mentioned to Dominic, "Guess who I saw at the library."

He stiffened, braced.

"That man, Finnig. You know. The one Kevin McBride asked to see if I was all right."

"Yes." Dominic relaxed. "We checked on him. He is a difficult man to put into a category."

"What do you mean by that?"

Dominic pushed up his lower lip, as he thought about how to reply. "Many strange people know him.

He appears to have a wide network that isn't really criminal. We can't find anything wrong about him, but he isn't—'' he chose to say in English ''—squeaky clean.'' Then he reverted to Italian. ''Do not encourage his attention.''

''I do not encourage any man's attention.''

''No?''

She amended her words. ''Yours.''

And Dominic smiled at her. ''Yes.''

But in the months that followed, she would see Finnig at the library as she was learning about recording children's books. She would see him sitting in a booth listening and speaking. She was certain that he was not recording for the public. But perhaps children understood his stilted manner of speech?

And she found out that the tape Benjamin loved had been made by... Tate Lambert.

With the proof of that before her, Fiona sat and thought for a while, then she managed to ask a new volunteer, ''When is Tate due back to record again?''

''Let me see.'' She got out a scheduling book, put it back and pulled another one. She hunted, blushing, saying, ''I'm new, you know. I can't always find things right away.''

''We are all beginners some time.'' Fiona soothed her.

''Ah, here we are. Tuesday. I believe she comes after she gets finished at the newspaper. About four. Did you want her to do a particular book?''

''No,'' Fiona said absently. So, Fiona realized, Tate was not only alive, she lived in Chicago. How strange. This woman who ignored her own child, taped books for other children.

And on a Tuesday night in August, as they shared their midnight snack, Fiona said to Dominic, "The tape that Benjamin said was his mother's voice? It is."

Dominic jerked. Then he simply stared.

"She lives." Fiona was sure.

"Yes."

"Doesn't she even see Benjamin?"

"No."

"Why not?" Fiona was very careful.

Dominic did not reply.

Fiona told him gently, "I saw her with children at the library and—"

Dominic became furious. She saw that he controlled himself with stern discipline. He put down his plate and cup to tread the floor in quick, pointless pacings.

She waited.

He turned to her finally, and asked, "What did she tell you?"

In his Italian, she replied formally, "I would not approach her without your permission, my lord." With her submissive words, she watched him levelly, as an equal. She was, by then, twenty-seven and more mature, but she still wore Dominic's slave bracelet on her ankle.

He made no comment and left the silence empty.

She asked, "Why would a woman ignore her child's birthday, but strain her day by coming to the library in the evening to read to other people's children?"

Dominic had no reply for that, either. But he looked at the bulge of their baby, and his conscience twisted in him with anguish.

In the morning, he said to Fiona, "I would ask you not to continue your work at the library." He looked at her in his most confident way. He expected her to submit.

She did not. "I enjoy my contribution. Do you realize that illiteracy is one of the nation's greatest problems? Anything that anyone can do is some help. We need more volunteers." She then had the audacity to mention, "You have a great voice. Children need to hear male voices. Their lives are filled with women. Would you volunteer?"

He knew about maneuvering, and she had just outmaneuvered him. "Fiona—"

"Good grief, feel this! He's going to be a street dancer."

Dominic put his hands on the baby stirring inside Fiona, and he frowned as the baby kicked. Then he leaned and kissed her stomach. "Poor tummy."

"Don't get fresh with a pregnant woman."

"Too pregnant?" he inquired with a slight smile.

"Not yet."

So another crisis was delayed. But Fiona could not put it off forever. She had to know, for Benjamin's sake. She was chipping away at Dominic. And it was after she overheard Tate say, "I have a little boy just your size," that she felt a great weight of guilt come down on her shoulders. Those were not the words of a shunning mother.

That night, she said to Dominic, "Does Tate know where Benjamin is?"

He stared in shock. "I will hear no more of this."

"You probably will. I need to understand."

His reply was to take his pillow and leave their room.

But Fiona picked up her own pillow and followed.

When she put it down on the bed in the spare room, where he lay so rigidly, he asked her with equal rigidity, "Why are you here?"

She replied logically, "I'm your wife. Just because I've displeased you, that isn't changed."

He really didn't want to quarrel, so he was silent.

As she settled into the bed with some difficulty, for it was by then September and she was seven months pregnant, she told him quite frankly, "You displease me, too, but I do love you, and I believe you're a good man. Stubborn. But basically good."

When he rose from the bed, she thought, I pushed too hard.

He said, "As long as we're going to sleep together, let's go back to our room."

Fiona didn't nag. She knew better than that. Days would go by before she would say something about Tate and ask him his opinion. "You knew her. Would she do this?"

"Leave it!"

She would look distressed and lay her hand on her growing stomach. "I cannot." She would sigh. "I need to understand."

Finally, Dominic told her, "My first wife was unfaithful. And my second wife left me. She was bored. I gave her everything. But she—left. She had no reason, no cause. She loved the boy. She was fascinated by him."

"You punished her. You won custody?"

Since he realized, at last, that that was exactly right, he was angry. "I will not discuss this. You are driving me crazy with your hounding at this. Benjamin has a good home. He is cared for."

With care, she asked, "But what about Tate? How could she be the woman she is, and not want contact with her own little boy?"

"It is none of your business." And he snarled the words. He stormed off to the other room, and again she followed, but he had locked the door. She knocked. He would not reply. In Italian, she said through the door, "I did not mean to take your room from you. I will not be there. You can return to it."

He lay a while, frowning, then he got up, unlocked the damned door and went back to their rooms. She was not there. She had said, "I will not be there." What did that mean? He called in a bellow, "Fiona?" as he tore through the house.

There were quick questionings, and Dominic snarled, "Where is she?"

"In the library," a shadow replied.

He stormed into the hall and through the house. He pulled open the door and found her wrapped in a blanket up to her nose, curled forlornly in his chair.

He said in a warning voice, "Don't try me too far."

And she replied, "There are limits to you."

He stopped and stared angrily at her, but he controlled himself. "Come to bed."

"I don't belong here. You have rejected me. I am tired of trying to placate you."

"Fiona," he warned.

"I have had enough. If you can storm off and leave me alone, then so can I be as childish. I will be at my parents' house. I will consider you more closely. I do not think you are ready to be a father. I will pick up Benjamin tomorrow. We will see you when you can discuss the questions that trouble me, in an adult manner."

He bellowed.

"I'll leave now. I will not endure this." But she had heard the pain in his sound.

Still she was committed, she put a bare foot to the floor, and he saw the slave bracelet. Oddly, that was what stopped his anger. Who did he think he was? My God, he thought, what am I doing to her? "Fiona—"

"Don't touch me." She walked to the door, and he stood helpless. She turned back to glance briefly at him, and she saw him sink to his knees and put his face in his hands. He said, "My God, help me."

She dropped the blanket and went to him to kneel in front of him and put her arms around his great shoulders. "Dominic. What is it? Why are you in such torment? It can't be because I am angry with you. Why are you suffering so?"

"I stole Benjamin from her. I have kept him. The court gave her custody. He is my son."

"She doesn't know where he is?" Fiona was appalled.

"I told her I had him."

"I am glad you at least did that. She must have been frantic. Thank you for trusting me with the truth. I could not understand. Now, I do. We will have to think on this. Come, my love, it's cold out here. Come to bed."

They did not sleep. They lay awake, but they held hands, each one's thinking separate. And one of her thoughts was that it had not embarrassed Dominic one iota that the shadows in the house had heard their quarrel, the men were that much a part of Dominic. But then she wondered about Benjamin.

The child had never forgotten his mother. How was all this for Benjamin? Seeing Tomas at the hospital,

Benjamin had wondered where he had been. What had become of Tomas? Benjamin must have wondered many times why he never saw his mother. He no longer asked. How had they explained it to him? But after all that time, about a year and a half, when he had first heard the tape, he had remembered his mother's voice. And he still played her tapes. Tapes. Without telling Dominic there were more than the first one, Fiona had gathered others for Benjamin's age. He now heard his mother reading seven books.

Although Fiona rarely spoke to Tate, she had observed her on occasion. And that October it was not really a surprise, when Finnig said to Fiona, "The husband d'Angelo, is his real name Lorenzo?"

She had stared at Finnig.

Finnig said, "You know Benjamin's mother. You see her here. She's a good woman. She ought to know the kid. Could I just take a couple of pictures of the boy? That's all she longs for. Just to see him in a picture. She hasn't seen him, now, for over two years."

That admonition put Fiona in a bind. She suffered. Could she go against Dominic? Could she agree to this? What would happen if Dominic took this baby and hid it away from its mother, Fiona? How would she survive that? Could she allow the pictures? She turned away from Finnig and did not reply.

He was there the next week. He asked, "Okay?"

And she replied, "I don't know."

He looked briefly at her stomach, which bulged out her coat, and he said, "It is almost time for you. You won't be around for a while after the baby comes. Tate is being married to a good man, Bill Sawyer. Give them this present of the boy's pictures."

"She's being married?"

"Yes. Her husband has had everyone trying to find Lorenzo. He is well-hidden."

"I will bring Benjamin here on Thursday. If you happen to take pictures . . ."

He involuntarily gave a quick, doubtful look at her stomach.

And the contractions began on Thursday morning. Fiona figured that was nerves. She was very careful. Romano, the father of eleven, was uncertain if she should go. When she was adamant that she needed to do that, Romano insisted on accompanying Nick as she and Benjamin went to the library. "Are you sure about going?" Romano asked doubtfully. "You are sure?"

And she replied, "I must."

Romano reluctantly decided to indulge her.

She did not see any photographer. And she didn't know if Finnig had managed to be there. So she went to the hospital at suppertime, not knowing if Tate would get the pictures or not. Then she had to think about herself and her own baby. But she really thought only of the baby.

Dominic was frantic. He was calm and his voice was soothing, but she could see that he was afraid. He told her, "You must be all right. I need you. I will do whatever you say about Benjamin. Tell me what you want."

And she panted the words. "Share him with Tate."

"I swear to you—"

But the doctor came in then, and said, "You're serious about having this baby. I thought you might wait a little longer. Ah-h, very good. Not long, now. Want to come along?"

Dominic said, "I need to be with her."

"You didn't take the classes," her doctor chided Dominic.

"I am a coward. I can't watch her hurt."

"Then how can you help her now? There must be twenty people down in the waiting room for this birth. They are crowding out everyone else. Is there some-one else to hold her hand... or yours?" He was jolly about it.

"No," said Dominic grimly. "I shall."

And Dominic did stay with Fiona. He was a sham-bles. The new little Lorenzo didn't look at all like the acrobat who had been bouncing around inside Fiona. He looked tiny and helpless. Dominic remembered when Benjamin had been born. He remembered Tate with her new baby.

"A very nice boy," the doctor bragged. "What will you name him?"

"Marcellus." Dominic was sure. "We shall call him Marc."

"Marcellus Lorenzo. Not English," commented the doctor.

Watching Fiona hold her son, Dominic agreed. "Italian."

And Fiona said sleepily, "Share Benjamin with Tate."

Dominic put it off. He was afraid to give up the boy because he might not get him back. But just after Thanksgiving, the man Finnig came to his office. That was a jolt. How had Finnig found him?

Dominic was a little stiff. Since he was always for-bidding with strangers, that meant that he was very hostile.

Finnig said, ' My name's Quintus Finnig. I know you checked me out."

"Yes."

"I love a woman whose sister is Tate Lambert Sawyer—"

"Sawyer?"

"She married Bill Sawyer at Thanksgiving time. She and her sister, Hillary, were married in a double wedding at the Lambert home down in Texas."

Finnig spoke very well in giving that information. Most of the words were clear. Dominic did not have to struggle unduly to understand.

Quint continued, "You haven't known the Lamberts, but you need for Benjamin to know them. They . . . grieve for him."

"Benjamin is my son."

"Yes. But would you see Bill Sawyer? I am his— em—emissary."

Dominic knew Bill Sawyer by reputation and he was almost joggled into incredulous laughter that Sawyer would use this street man as a go-between. But then Quintus Finnig began the "sell."

"Your Italian God is my Irish God. He understands you for He, too, had a Son."

That was the beginning. And Quint leaned back and the two diverse men talked. As Quint became more comfortable with Dominic, his language was more of the street, but the weaving of words from the Irishman wasn't that different from those of the Italian.

Dominic agreed if the new husband of Tate was a good man, he would allow Tate to at least see Benjamin. Bill Sawyer was to call on Dominic at his office.

Dominic and Finnig stood and shook hands. As he did that, Finnig said, "You're a law-abiding man."

As Finnig had calculated, those last words did niggle inside Dominic's conscience.

* * *

It was just before Christmas when Tate's new husband, Bill Sawyer, finally met with Dominic Lorenzo. The new snow was clean, and the holiday air was over all of the city. The Salvation Army officers rang the bells on the street corners, and the cold wind hurried people along.

When Dominic's secretary courteously escorted Bill to his office, Dominic rose from his chair and stood with equal courtesy.

Bill said, "I understand congratulations are in order. Your wife and new son are doing well?"

"Yes," replied Dominic somewhat stiffly. "Thank you. Sit down. Please." The "please" was tacked on; it sounded so, even to Dominic.

Bill sat and waited.

Dominic said, "I am hearing that you searched for me. I hear it from all quarters. Was it only for the boy?"

"Tate's boy."

"And mine."

Bill was silent.

Dominic admitted, "Tate had custody of Benjamin. I did wrong in taking him. Fiona has made me promise to give him back to Tate. Do you want him?" Dominic turned, and seemed to assess Bill's reaction.

Bill was surprised and smiled. He stood up and reached to shake hands with Dominic. "Quite frankly, you had me over a barrel. You could have demanded almost anything of me."

"Ah," said Dominic. "I wish I'd known." Then he added pensively, "I shall miss the boy."

"I'm sure Tate will be generous about giving you time with Benjamin." He added tellingly, "She will know how you want to see him."

"Tell her I am sorry. I hadn't thought she would grieve for him. Finnig told me."

"How do you know Finnig?"

"By surprise," Dominic admitted. "An interesting character. I can find nothing wrong with his operations."

"Nor can we. When may Tate see Benjamin? When can we have him?"

Painfully, Dominic admitted, "I find this very hard. He is such a nice little boy. I'm very proud of him."

"These kinds of things are very tough. I have a daughter—"

"Finnig told me about that. I know of your ex-wife."

Bill was again silent.

"Well—" Dominic seemed awkward "—I don't quite know what to say. Will you contact me? To tell me if I can see Benjamin? Could he visit us sometime? My wife has become very attached to him. That's why her heart was so soft for Tate, and she worried about her. Then she learned how Tate grieved . . . yes," he said, acknowledging that Tate's grief had touched him.

"I'll ask Tate," Bill promised.

"Thank you."

"You've done the right thing. I believe I can guess what this has cost you."

"Yes. Here is my address." Dominic handed Bill a card. "I might suggest you visit several times and have him visit you before we move him to your place. I'm not sure anyone knows exactly how to do this to a child. He cried for his mother for a long time after I took him."

The two men shook hands, as if for a formal agreement. But Dominic stood with his head down as Bill left.

Fiona had left Benjamin in his room, but she watched nervously. She saw the strange car drive up and her excitement was high. She checked on Marc, who slept like an angel, and she hovered to listen for the door. She was there as soon as Tate came to the door, and Fiona opened it. She said to Tate, "At last."

Tate hugged her. "Finnig told me how much you tried to help me."

Fiona's soft laugh was filled with sympathy. "That Finnig, he does try to save the world. I'm glad he helped you. Benjamin is a dear child."

"Where—"

Fiona smiled kindly, but her eyes were teary. "This way."

Bill asked Tate, "Would it be better if I waited here?"

"No, come with me."

Fiona took Tate's hand, as if Tate were younger and needed leading. They went down the hall to a door, and Fiona tapped on the portal.

A little voice called, "Come in."

Fiona opened the door, and Benjamin turned around from his cars on the floor. Seeing guests, he stood up to say, "Hello."

Fiona said, "This is your mama."

Alone, Tate walked several steps into the room and sank to her knees as Benjamin watched with interest.

He said, "No. Mama here." He went to a tape player, took Tate's tape and put it into the machine.

Tate was silent.

Benjamin explained the voice. "Mama."

Tate told her son, "That is I. Listen to my voice. I read that book to you." She opened her purse and took out a little book and held it out to him. "I used to read this to you."

"My book! That's my book." He came to her and took the well-used little book into his hands. "Mine!" He grinned and hugged the book. "Read to me." And he sat down on Tate's knees, to lean back against her as if he had done that just yesterday.

All three adults were undone.

Fiona tiptoed away, leaving the couple with the child. She went to their room, where Dominic had stayed. He could not bear to watch the drama unfolding in his house. He turned his anguished face to Fiona and his words were Italian. "I cannot do this."

"Oh, my love. Now you know Tate's suffering. But you will not lose Benjamin. We will see him. He will know us and Marc." And Fiona saw that Dominic wept.

His tears rent her very being. She said softly, "Ah, for Benjamin to have two people who love him so unselfishly."

Huskily, Dominic disclaimed that. "I am selfish."

Fiona put her arms around him and leaned against him. "No, darling, you are not. You are only stubborn. And I love you above all else in this world. God should smile on you for what you have done today."

* * * * *

From the popular author of the bestselling title
DUNCAN'S BRIDE (Intimate Moments #349)
comes the

LINDA HOWARD COLLECTION

Two exquisite collector's editions that contain four of
Linda Howard's early passionate love stories. To add
these special volumes to your own library, be sure
to look for:

VOLUME ONE: *Midnight Rainbow*
Diamond Bay
(Available in March)

VOLUME TWO: *Heartbreaker*
White Lies
(Available in April)

Silhouette Books®

SLH92

Take 4 bestselling love stories FREE

Plus get a FREE surprise gift!

Special Limited-time Offer

Mail to Silhouette Reader Service™

In the U.S.
3010 Walden Avenue
P.O. Box 1867
Buffalo, N.Y. 14269-1867

In Canada
P.O. Box 609
Fort Erie, Ontario
L2A 5X3

YES! Please send me 4 free Silhouette Special Edition® novels and my free surprise gift. Then send me 6 brand-new novels every month, which I will receive months before they appear in bookstores. Bill me at the low price of $2.96* each—a savings of 43¢ apiece off the cover prices. There are no shipping, handling or other hidden costs. I understand that accepting the books and gift places me under no obligation ever to buy any books. I can always return a shipment and cancel at any time. Even if I never buy another book from Silhouette, the 4 free books and the surprise gift are mine to keep forever.

*Offer slightly different in Canada—$2.96 per book plus 69¢ per shipment for delivery. Canadian residents add applicable federal and provincial sales tax. Sales tax applicable in N.Y.

235 BPA ADMC   335 BPA ADMQ

Name	(PLEASE PRINT)
Address	Apt. No.
City	State/Prov. Zip/Postal Code.

This offer is limited to one order per household and not valid to present Silhouette Special Edition® subscribers. Terms and prices are subject to change.

SPED-92   © 1990 Harlequin Enterprises Limited

Silhouette Special Edition®

You loved the older sister in
The Cowboy's Lady
You adored the younger sister in
The Sheriff Takes a Wife
Now get a load of the brothers in
DEBBIE MACOMBER'S new trilogy.

THOSE MANNING MEN

starting in March 1992 with a believable

MARRIAGE OF INCONVENIENCE

Jamie Warren's new secret marriage to Rich Manning was strictly
a matter of convenience—a legal, acceptable way for Jamie to
have a baby before time ran out. And it *was* convenient—terribly
convenient—until they fell in love....

Look for more books by Debbie Macomber, chronicling the lives
and loves of THOSE MANNING MEN, this May and July in your
local bookstore. Only in Special Edition.

SEMAN-1